Strip It Down

The
Heart and Soul
of
Riley and Jace

P.D. Fitzgerald

authorHOUSE®

AuthorHouse™
1663 Liberty Drive
Bloomington, IN 47403
www.authorhouse.com
Phone: 1 (800) 839-8640

Published by AuthorHouse 06/22/2016

ISBN: 978-1-5246-1544-4 (sc)
ISBN: 978-1-5246-1543-7 (e)

Chapter 1

It's the middle of December in River Falls, Louisiana. The weather here is like a box of chocolates, you never now what you're gonna get. It could be sunny and seventy-five degrees or windy and cold with the low in the upper thirties. Today we are somewhere in the middle and its pouring down rain.

I'm running late, it's already seven thirty and I still have to do my hair and drive across town to be at the work by eight. I've been with KWRB broadcasting for six years. The Radio station is small; we only have fifteen employees including myself. We all consider each other as family especially Sara and I. We're two peas in a pod. Our personalities are alike in so many ways and we are always looking out for each other. I call the station to tell Sara I'm running a little behind but I'm on my way. I get half way to the station before I realize I forgot my umbrella. The rain is not letting up in the least. I think to my self it's going to be one of those days where nothing and everything is going to happen.

I pull into the parking lot; all the spots are full, except the very last one. I'm going to be soaked before I make it inside but I gather my things and run to the door of the station, only to see Sara laughing uncontrollably. She opens the door and in a sarcastic tone I ask, "What might you find so funny?"

"You," she said, "you look like a drenched rat but a cute drenched rat."

"Well then, that makes it all better; I hope my clients think so," I reply.

"They make these things called umbrellas that keep you dry," mumbled Sara, "you should get one!"

"I see you have jokes this morning," I said, "I was in a hurry and left mine at home, genius."

"I see someone woke up on the wrong side of the bed," said Sara.

"I'm sorry if I seem a little snappy, I just can't catch a break this morning. Not only did I forget to set my alarm but I also have a meeting with a new client. I still have to prepare my notes. Never mind the fact I look like I just took a shower with my clothes on and my hair looks like a birds nest."

I head to my office to prepare my proposal and Sara comes around the corner, "Today aren't you meeting with the one and only Jace Carmichael?"

"Yes I am" I replied " Yes I am"

"Well don't let him intimidate you," as she turns to walk to the break room.

"Wait a minute, is there something you want to tell me?" as I leap from my chair to chase her down the hall.

Laughing she reminds me that every sales person on the planet have tried to convince Jace Carmichael to advertise on the radio. All ends with no luck. Not to mention the fact he has a way of making you feel like a complete loser stripping you of all self worth by the time you leave. "He has a way of intimidating you just with his presence and demeanor," said Sara.

"Oh my God stop already! I'm already a nervous wreck! Now I just want to hide in the corner and rock back and forth. You Sara Hall are no help!" I blurt out.

"But I am still your best friend!" she hollers.

"Well I can't deny that," whispering under my breath.

"I have faith in you Riley, if anyone can lock him down, it's you! So stop stressing. I'll see you at lunch. You better hurry, you have an hour drive and don't be a babbling idiot."

I grab my things and take off. I was already on edge but thanks to Sara, I feel like I'm walking into the lion's den with a pork chop tied around my neck. I can already feel the churning and dread in my stomach. I'm overwhelmed with intimidation and haven't even come face to face with the man of steel. From the stories I've heard, I will need kryptonite to bring him down to my level. I decide not to let it worry me and turn up the music for the drive.

That's my way of escaping life, music and writing. I could be stranded on an island with just a pen and paper and get lost in my thoughts, deep as an ocean Sara would say. So being in radio suites me well. I get to use my imagination writing commercials for clients and be the voice that entertains thousands of listeners. I'm not as enthusiastic about being in sales as I am about being a DJ though. That's only because in sales I have to deal with the public and I am not one to enjoy the spot light. I would much rather be behind the scenes. The best part about being a DJ is you can hear me, but you can't see me. My favorite song comes on and I start singing at the top of my lungs. I have my favorites but being I am music buff, I know the lyrics to every song.

I get lost in my own world and time slips away. Before I know it I'm sitting in the parking lot of Carmichael's Construction. The building is much bigger than I had expected. The nerves take back over and in a panic I grab my things and take off. I get inside and the hallway seems to go for miles. I thought that by the time I get where I'm supposed to be I won't be able to breathe to propose anything.

My thoughts are going a million different directions; the stress is back in full force. *What if I say the wrong thing or he instantly rips me to shreds before I can even say a word?* I'm in total panic mode at this point and begin talking to myself to calm down. *Riley get it together! You're going to do fine just stay focused and breathe.* I glance at my watch to check the time. I definitely don't want to be late for my own slaying. I pick up my pace to a brisk walk. I look down to straighten my blouse and make sure I look presentable. The next thing I know, I'm sitting on the ground dazed and confused. My proposal scattered across the floor. I look up to see what just ran me over and I could not believe my eyes.

Standing before me was nothing shy of a tall glass of sweet tea on a smoldering hot summer day. He was tall and built like a gladiator. It looked like the sun had kissed his skin. His thick jet-black hair and precisely trimmed goatee made his green eyes look like emeralds. I thought I had died and gone to heaven! Unfortunately, he killed my dream and quickly brought me back to reality. "You might want to pick that up and next time, watch where you're going!" He showed no compassion and without even the slightest concern he continued on his way. I'm not sure if I'm more embarrassed about the slobber running down my chin or the total look of disorientation on my face or maybe even both. I began gathering my work and thinking that man was the devil in sheep's clothing. He definitely won't win the award for Mr. Personality. I'm still mumbling under my breath when I get to the front counter. I introduce myself to the receptionist; "I'm Riley Davis with KWRB. I have an appointment with Mr. Carmichael."

"I'm Katie it's nice to finally meet you," she said, "he's expecting you. Go down the hall, second door on the left." I get to the door and take a minute to collect myself. I take a deep breath and before I can knock I hear this earth shaking demand, "Come in!"

Instantly alarm bells go off. I know that voice. This can't be happening, I think to myself. I open the door with a glimpse of hope that I'm wrong but standing before me is none other than Mr.

Personality himself. I reach out my hand to introduce myself, "Hi Mr. Carmichael! I'm Riley Davis with KW..."

"I know who you are," cutting me off before I can say another word. "I don't like to waste my time. So tell me, Ms. Davis, what makes you think you have something I need? I have been in business for ten years and never once used advertising. I have been very successful thus far. I don't see how you could benefit me in any way, matter fact you may need my business, but I don't need yours. I expect you will make this quick and be on your way."

I'm sure I look like a scolded puppy as I sat quietly allowing him to rant but this smirk on my face is hiding my rising blood pressure. I'm ready to pluck them emerald eyes right out of their socket and where them around my neck. I sigh and look him dead in the eye.

"Are you always this full of sunshine, Mr. Carmichael, or is today my lucky day?"

I totally caught him off guard and the look on his face was priceless.

I guess everyone is so intimidated by him that they clam up and are left speechless, but not me. I'm known to be stubborn and a rebel at times.

"I didn't earn my fortune by pacifying people like you Riley," he snarls. "I worked hard to make something of myself so I wouldn't have to be a salesman or door greeter like everyone else." Heaven help me this man thinks he's God! I have listened to him belittle me long enough. I slide my proposal to his side of the desk.

"You are absolutely right Mr. Carmichael! You seem to have it all under control and I won't waste your time. I will say this though, all good things come to an end and with your greater than thou attitude and arrogant personality your luck should be thin as ice! Tell me Mr. Carmichael, what makes you think you are so special anyway? You bleed just like me. Now you sir have a good day!"

The slamming of the door echoed down the hall and there I was taking the walk of shame. I'm usually pretty good at holding my tongue but this man's arrogant attitude drives me wild. My emotions are in over drive and I could almost cry. Who does this man think he is treating people like they're nothing? I can tell you this, he doesn't know who he's messing with. I, Riley Davis, love a challenge, and Carmichael Construction hasn't seen the last of me yet!

I make my way to my Jeep. She wasn't anything fancy but she got me where I needed to go and I was ok with that. I throw my things inside turning the key. The battery is dead. No, no, no not here, not now! I lean my head against the steering wheel and pray for a miracle. *Jesus please don't make me have to go back in there and ask for help.* I try it again and nothing. I know I have no choice but to go back inside. I will ask to borrow some jumper cables and steer clear of Mr. Carmichael at all cost. I get to the front counter and before I can say a word Katie just smiles and points outside. I turned around to see what she was pointing at and there he stood leaning against the hood with his arms crossed. "What is this torture?" I utter underneath my breath. You just have to deal with him long enough to get back on the road, I tell myself. I keep what composure I have left and head toward the vehicle. The first thing out of his mouth is nothing I want to hear.

"You drive this thing? It has to be at least ten years old. Why don't you buy something newer?"

I instantly reply, "Matter fact, I do and it's only six years old. Thank you!"

"What's the problem, what's wrong with it?" he asks.

"I think the battery is dead," I reply, "Do you have some cables I can borrow?"

You would have thought I asked the man to change the oil or something. He has this mean mug look, where he pouches his lips and crinkles his forehead.

"I'll call road side assistance. That's what it's for. Will that work for you?"

"That would be great Mr. Carmichael, or you could fly me back in your private jet, whichever's more convenient for you."

I think we both realize we have met our match. Neither one of us is going to intimidate the other or let it show anyway. We both stood there in complete silence so I decided to break the awkwardness looming in the air.

"It wouldn't hurt you to smile once in a while and it might even make more people like you."

He tried not to react but there it was this huge grin.

"You, Ms. Davis, are something else!"

I return his smile and say, "You can call me Riley." I know there is this softer side hidden behind that facade, I can sense it. The service man gets old Betsey started and I thank them both. I turn to open the door; he grabs it and holds it shut. Then in a subtle tone he said, "You can call me Jace."

Chapter 2

The New Year seems to be starting off on a good note. Sara and I are hanging out at our favorite place, Mackie's Bar and Grill. It's small and cozy, surrounded by big mossy oak trees sitting on the banks of the Louisiana bayou. We like sitting on the patio and watching the lights dance across the water as we talk about everyday life. Tonight we are waiting to see the firework display and discussing our New Years Resolutions. When out of nowhere Sara asked, "Have you heard from Mr. Carmichael?"

I almost choked, coughing up a lung.

"No, and I don't expect to! I wrote that account off the minute that I returned to the station. I'm certain I'm the last person Jace Carmichael wants to see!"

"I've never seen you give up on something so easily Riley! He must have ripped you to shreds," said Sara.

"You have no idea," I blurt, "the man is like a bear! I'm not talking about a care bear either."

"The things that come out of your mouth, you keep me laughing. By the way, how did you get out of your shift tonight?" she asked.

"I didn't, I prerecorded everything so people assume I'm there. Isn't technology great?"

"I like to listen to you and all your philosophies about life. The passion in your voice has a way of drawing people in," said Sara.

"You're bias," I reply.

"We are both stars in our own right and I think you are absolutely amazing!" she exclaims.

We decide to call it a night, we could both use some rest before things at work become too hectic. This is a busy time of year for advertising. All the company's budgets are up for renewal and we both have our hands full. A couple weeks go by and out of nowhere I receive an email:

> *Riley,*
> *I have reconsidered looking over your proposal and would like to meet you for lunch to go over the details. We can discuss arrangements regarding the*

*place and time on a conference call. I have included
my cell number and will be looking forward to
hearing from you.
Sincerely,
Jace Carmichael
(551) 117-0824*

It's past five o'clock and I don't want to call after business hours. I decide to wait until morning before I reply. I'm in a rush to get home because I have a few things I need to take care of before I head back to work. I rummage through the mail and grab a snack before I head back to the station. I look over the playlist scheduled for my shift and pull a current weather update. I have a few extra minutes to spare so I run to the break room grab something to drink and head back to my cell. I call it that because it reminds me of a padded room they use for crazy people. Like the ones you see on TV, sound proof with padding all over the walls. The only difference is I have a microphone and soundboard.

The first thing in the lineup is the station ID, KWRB 107.1 the Wave and then I'm on Que.

"It's a great evening here in West Central Louisiana. We have clear skies tonight and the best music coming your way so kick back, relax and stay tuned. This is Riley and I'll be taking your calls till midnight."

I really like what I do! I hear people's stories about falling in love or how they're discouraged with everyday life. I give advice and sometimes I just listen. My favorite part is picking out the perfect song to fit the situation. I receive calls all evening requesting songs and I throw in a couple of my favorites before the night is over.

The next morning, I'm running behind schedule. Last night's shift seemed longer than usual and I didn't get much rest. I rehearsed the call to Jase over and over in the back of my mind. I don't want to get my hopes up. What if things go south? Mr. Personality really knows how to jerk my chain! I never let my guard down completely for anything, life has graciously taught me better. I dial the number on the bottom of the email and on the second ring it picks up, "Jace speaking."

"Good morning Mr. Carmichael! It's Riley Davis. I understand you would like to take another look at my proposal?"

"Yes, I would, can we meet for lunch? It's on me." I try to hide the excitement in my voice; I don't want to boost his ego any bigger than it already is. "I will look at my schedule. What did you have in mind?" I ask.

"Monday twelve o'clock, wherever you choose. I will come to you," he said.

"There is this nice place down by the river called Mackie's, they have the best lunch specials. I can meet you there," I reply.

"That sounds great, I'll see you then and I'm glad you called," he states.

I immediately hang up and call Sara. "You're not going to believe what just happened! Guess who invited me to lunch to go over his proposal?"

"I have no clue," she said, "but don't keep me in suspense."

I can't contain myself any longer and blurt out, "Jace Carmichael! He's meeting me Monday at Mackie's."

"No way! How did you pull that off?" she asked.

"I have no idea! Maybe standing up to him wasn't such a bad thing after all. I just might reel him in yet!" I reply.

"I knew you could do it Riley! I think I'm going to act like an ass with my clients, since it worked so well for you!" We both burst into laughter.

"You're crazy Sara! This is pure luck, nothing more," I reply.

I get up extra early Monday. I want to make a better impression this time. I decide on my black suite with a turquoise color dress shirt; the shirt complements my sandy blonde hair and blue green eyes. I can't decide on which pair of shoes to wear, flats or heels? I have a complex since I'm already six-feet tall but go with the heels anyway. I put on my silver necklace and earrings then add some shimmering pink lipstick to top it all off. I stop by the station and glance over my notes while I chat with Sara.

"Riley, you look great! Are you nervous?" Sara asked.

"I'm ok, this should be a breeze compared to the first encounter. I know what to expect this time and I'm going to kill him with kindness," I say smirking.

"Good luck! I'll be praying for you," said Sara.

I get to Mackie's and inform the waiter of my reservations. He leads me out to the patio and sitting there is Jace in a grey suit and red tie, staring out over the water. He might have a bad attitude but he sure looks picture perfect! The suit is tailored to fit him like a glove; I was stripping him down with my eyes unveiling what possibly lay underneath. He either felt the burning of my stare or caught a glimpse of me out of the corner of his eye. He stands up and straightens his suit saying, "Hello Riley! How are you?"

"Doing well Mr. Carmichael," I reply.

We both take our seats as I put my proposal on the table. I order some water with lemon and he does the same. I need something to wash down this lump in my throat from all the nerves.

"So tell me Riley, what made you choose the radio business?" he asked.

"Let's see, I really like singing and music, but singing was not my forte. I sound more like a dying cat and will never earn a spot in the angel's choir. I decided it was best if I stuck with the later of the two," I said smiling. "What made you choose the construction business?"

"My father was in construction and watching him growing up, I knew I didn't want to be a laborer the rest of my life. I went to college for a degree in business and started Carmichael's Construction. I'm more interested in learning about you Riley. I already know you're fearless and out spoken," he said with a grin. "Tell me, where did you get them blue eyes? How old are you? Are you married? Do you live around here?"

"If I would have known I was going to be under interrogation Mr. Carmichael, I would have made some notes." My sarcasm is followed by huge smile. "Let's see, I look like my father and I have my mother's eyes. I'm twenty-eight years old and my birthday is in November. I was born in Dallas, Texas. I moved here at the age of nine. My parents are both deceased. I've been on my own since I was sixteen. I'm not in a relationship at the moment, and I live a couple miles from the station. That sir is my story."

"There's something mysterious about you Riley. I find you very intriguing," he replied. I can feel the warmth in my face as I began to blush.

"I'm really quite simple," I reply, "tell me about yourself, what's your story?"

"I'm thirty-seven years old and my birthdays in August. I've been married for six years and have a seven-year-old daughter. I was born and raised in Jones Town, Louisiana and built my business from the ground up. The rest is history," he said.

The way we interacted made it seem like we had known each other for years. The instant connection between us was magnetic.

We are so caught up in our conversation with each other that hours had passed before I notice the time.

"It's three-twenty! I have a meeting at four o'clock with Denise from Candy Connections on the other side of town. I know if I don't leave now, I won't make it on time." I tell him, and start gathering my things. Then I realize we never even discussed the business proposal. Before I could mention it he said, "Write me a commercial and I'll come by the station and sign the contract." He walks me to my car leading me with one hand in the small of my back.

"I really enjoyed your company Riley. I'm already looking forward to seeing you again, you know to hear the commercial, of course," he said with a smile. There's something about this man that keeps me off guard and twisted. He makes my insides tremble and my palms sweaty.

"Oh yes, the commercial," I reply as I fumble around in my purse for my keys. "I will take care of that first thing and have it ready upon your arrival."

The man I met in my first encounter was not the same man I've come to know. This man is smart, intriguing, funny and kind. There is gentleness hidden behind his coat of armor. We are both drawn to each other, there's no denying that!

Chapter 3

Jace and I have been spending a lot of time together over the last four months. We talk on the phone everyday and see each other all week. He drives down and we have a picnic at the park or meet at Mackie's for dinner. His whole life has been in the spotlight, climbing the ladder to success. Somewhere, along the way, he has lost his self in the hustle of everyday life. I on the other hand, am the complete opposite. You get what you see! To me it's not about material things in life. It's about what's inside. We obviously come from opposite sides of the spectrum. I'm like a Motel 6 and he's the Hampton but together we find common ground.

I get a call from Jace in the middle of my shift asking if I could come to his office.

"I know it's late but there's something I want to show you!" he said.

I've gotten really good at recording so I can spend more time with him.

"It will take me a little while," I reply.

"Hurry up! I'll be waiting for you and I'm not good with patience," he jokes.

"It's time you learn some, I will be there soon." When I get to the front of his office, he's waiting outside. I immediately ask, "Why are you standing in the dark?"

"You ask too many questions," he said, "follow me!"

We go around to the back of the building and he points to the fire escape. "You made me drive all this way to show me the fire escape?" I ask.

"No we're going to use that to get to the roof," he said with a huge grin.

I'm thinking he has lost his mind at this point. "This better be good, Jace Carmichael!"

"Just go Riley! I'm right behind you," he said in a dominating voice.

I can tell he spends a lot of time here. There's a blanket, a radio, and a half-empty can of coke.

"This is where I come when I want to escape the world," he states as he lay down on the blanket, putting his arms behind his head.

"Don't be afraid, I won't bite!" patting the other side of the blanket.

I lie next to him and look up, the still of the night is captivating. The moon is under siege by the stars. Their twinkling glow looks like a blanket of fireflies covering the heavens.

"It's amazing up here, the view is breathtaking Jase," I say.

"I lay here and get lost in the still of night, seeking solitude," he whispered. "I knew you would like it. I can picture you sitting here writing your poetry under the moonlight. The way you describe everything with such depth and passion is beautiful."

"That's how I escape. I take what I feel and transcribe it into words. Some people see life through rose colored glasses, but I feel it, and you, Jace, stir my soul."

We lie side by side and gaze at the stars. It seemed as though we were the only two people on the planet.

"Do you know where the Big Dipper is?" he asked. He points them out, describing each one in detail as if he had hung them himself. We dwell in the desire to know all there is to know about each other.

"What did you want to be growing up?" I ask.

"An Optometrist. The eyes are the window to the soul," he replied.

"What do you see when you look in mine?" I asked.

"An angel, Riley Davis. I see an angel. You bring color to my world." He puts his arm under my head and pulls me close. "What about you?" he asked.

"A physiologist. I'm intrigued by what makes crazy people like you tick," I said laughing.

"Well what have you figured out?" he asked with a smile.

"I have come to the conclusion that I want to be part of your madness," I whisper softly.

It's in the early morning hours. Lost in the still of the night, we drift off into a quiet slumber. I'm not sure how long Jace has been awake before I hear him say, "Riley wake up!" I open my eyes and he is leaning over me gently sweeping my hair from my face. His hands are big and strong, yet they caress me with utter tenderness. I'm still in a daze and not sure if I'm dreaming.

"Its late sunshine, get up!" he said.

I realize this is no dream. Startled, I quickly sit up.

"Oh my God! What time is it?" I ask with confusion.

I grab my phone and look at the clock, it's a little past nine. I immediately call the station.

"This is Riley. I'm not feeling well and won't be able to make it in today."

I hang up and run my hands through my hair. I'm still not completely coherent and I'm trying to grasp the concept of how I let this happen. *I'm never this careless and irresponsible!* I think to myself.

"You don't look sick to me, a hot mess maybe, but not sick. Matter of fact I thought I was in a nightmare when I rolled over and saw you there," Jace blurts out. "I almost jumped over the ledge till I realized it was just you," he said laughing.

"Really? I guess you think your all that? Tuck your shirt in, you look like a slob," I said grinning from ear to ear.

He takes me by the hand and pulls me close. Our eyes lock as he runs his fingers through my hair.

"I'm sorry you missed work Riley. I didn't mean for that to happen, but I'm not sorry for the time we spent together," he whispers.

Our eyes never lose contact and while holding my face in the palm of his hands he gently kisses my forehead. My knees are weak and chills are creeping up my spine. *Be still my heart!* I tell myself

I know I'm in trouble if I don't leave now. I have to fight this desire. *It's wrong, he's a married man!* I tell myself. I break eye contact and tell him I have to go. I turn to walk away and he grabs my arm saying, "Spend the day with me Riley. I have a cabin by the river. We can do anything you want."

"I wish I could Jace, but I don't think that's a good idea. I need to head back home I have some calls to make and appointments I need to reschedule," I reply.

"You're breaking my heart," he pleads, "at least let me pay you for a day's work."

"I don't need your money. I have my own, but I may need a therapist if I keep hanging out with you," I said laughing. "You drive me crazy!"

I can't stop thinking about Jace the entire drive home. The thoughts inside my head are playing tug of war with my emotions. I'm torn between right and wrong. I justify what we are doing with the scenario we are just friends. Deep down I'm not fooling myself. I can't seem to get enough of this man nor do I want to. I tell myself I have enough self-control and respect that I would never cross that line.

I had only been home for a short time when I here a knock at the door. I already know its Sara; I just wasn't sure how long it would be before she showed up.

"I just wanted to stop by and check on you," she states, as I open the door.

"I'm ok now," I reply, "I just wasn't feeling very well this morning."

"Come on Riley, spit it out! What is up? Where have you been? On my way to work I noticed you weren't home," she stated.

I was hesitant to tell Sara where I was because I wasn't sure what she would think about it. I definitely didn't want her to think badly of me.

"I was with Jace," I say. "Nothing happened, we just lost track of time and fell asleep."

The look on Sara's face was a mixture of shock and disbelief.

"What! You stayed the night with Jace? Riley! What are you thinking? Have you lost your mind?" she states.

"I know what you're thinking Sara," bowing my head in shame, "but it's not like that. We are just good friends, that's all."

"Who are you trying to convince yourself or me Riley? It's written all over your face!" she exclaims. "You're falling for him. Your eyes sparkle like diamonds whenever you say his name. I just don't want to see you get hurt! Be careful Riley, you're playing with fire."

"I have it under control," I said to Sara, but deep down inside I'm not so sure.

The evening starts off pretty quiet and then the phone lights up.

"The wave 107.1. What's on your mind tonight?" I answer. I was totally caught of guard and unaware of the conversation I was about to have. The gravel in his voice was an instant give away.

"I would like to request a song," he said.

What is he doing? I ask myself.

"What can I play for you this evening?" I ask.

"I met this girl and she's something special. I can't get her off of my mind. I was wondering if you could play *I Want to Know* to make her understand how I feel," he replied.

I'm trying hard to keep my composure, but you can hear the crack in my voice.

"I can do that for you, what's her name?" I ask.

"I call her angel. That's what I see when I look in her eyes," he said.

I swallow the lump in my throat and take a deep breath to slow my racing heart; it's going so fast that wild horses couldn't keep up. I thank him for calling and announce his request.

"If you're listening tonight, Angel, this one's for you."

I start the song and immerse myself into the lyrics. I hang onto every word and wonder if he has any clue that I am falling for him fast. The next afternoon I receive a text from Jace:

I will be going out of town for a few days and would like to see you before I leave. We can spend Saturday together at the cabin. I will pick you up.

I ponder for some time before I answer. The struggle between right and wrong begins a battle in my mind. Although the conviction is strong, my desire to be in his presence wins.

Chapter 4

The log cabin sits on top of a hill, nestled deep in the woods, and is surrounded by Oak trees. The grassy moss drapes across their limbs like tasseled hair. The wrap around porch and old rocking chairs add to its beauty and charm. Down by the water's edge, there's an old pier, gently swaying from the current in the midst of the Calico Bayou. The summer heat could melt a candle, but today the sky is overcast and there's a drizzling rain to quench the thirst of the southern heat. I was caught up in the beauty of my surroundings when Jace clears his throat. "Are you going to just stand there or come inside?"

"What? Are you scared you might melt? I love the rain. It cleanses the spirit," I said, with a giggle.

I take his hand and we walk down to the pier.

"Relax Jace. Close your eyes and feel the rain wash over you."

He takes off his shirt, lays back and closes his eyes. I watched intensely as each drop danced across his body and rolled down his chest. Accumulating between the ripples in his stomach, intimately touching parts of him, I could only dream of.

"Why are you so quiet? What are you thinking?" he asked.

"That I'm jealous of the rain!" I mumbled, jumping into the water.

I had to do something to contain this fire burning inside me. He jumps in after me and pulls me close, "Close your eyes. I want you to feel what I feel," he said softly.

He tangles his hand in my hair and with a gentle tug tilts my head back. He uses the other hand to trace the outline of my lips. I can feel his breath on my skin causing my body to erupt with chills. The magic in his touch paralyzed me, leaving my body limp in his arms yearning for more. He pressed his lips to mine exploding with passion, causing my insides to quiver. The taste of desire immensely lingers as he softly whispers, "I'm falling in love with you, Riley!" I can't utter a word. I'm captivated and lost in this moment. Overwhelmed by my emotions that I can no longer contain. Escaping, a single tear rolls down my cheek. He puts his forehead against mine. Our bodies are aching with passion. We stand in silence, exhausted from the power and intensity that dwells from within.

There's a storm brewing in the distance and the rolling thunder demands our attention. "Let's get you inside. I have some clothes you can wear," he said. He shows me where I can change, handing me a white long sleeve button down shirt, a pair of sweatpants and some socks. The smell of his cologne is woven into the fabric of the shirt. I take a deep breath and let it surround my senses. I towel dry my hair and head to the living room to find Jace. "Well look at you. You look quite business like. I may have to hire you as my personal assistant," he said with a huge smile.

"You do want to stay in business right? I was thinking I look more like a bum!" I reply, as we both start laughing.

He pulls me down on the couch, "Lay with me for a while before we have to leave. I will be out of town next week and without you, it seems like a lifetime." He wraps his arms around me and lays his head next to mine. "I'll call you every chance I get. If you need something, Riley, you can call me."

My head is buried in his chest and the beating of his heart serenades mine.

"I don't want to leave," I mumble.

I could stay wrapped in his arms forever. I feel so loved; in his arms is where I belong. I've put it off long enough.

"We need to go, it's getting late and we have a long drive home." He helps me gather my things as I whisper softly, "I'm going to miss you Jace!" The entire ride home I was overcome with sadness.

I could no longer fool myself. I was in love with someone that could never be mine. I tried to conceal my thoughts by staring out the window but Jace could read me like a book.

"What's on your mind, Riley? Talk to me," he said.

Where would I begin? You're married and I'm in love with you! I thought to myself.

"I'm ok I'm just tired that's all," I reply.

What he doesn't know is I'm trying to figure out how to let go while I still can. I realize if I don't do it now, I never will. How do you walk away from the one thing that makes you feel alive? He walks me to the door and helps me put my things inside.

"I will call you tomorrow once I get settled in the hotel. I'm going to miss you Cinderella," he said with a chuckle.

"I was thinking more like Beauty and the Beast," I said laughing. "I miss you already!"

Once he leaves emptiness fills me. I try not to think about what I have to do, but it haunts me and I can't sleep. I'm completely tortured between what I'm feeling and what's right. I decide I will not take his calls while he's gone and will give his account to Sara. If I cut off all contact before long I will just be a memory.

The next evening Sara asks me to go to Mackie's to have a couple drinks with her and Keith. We met Keith five years ago. He is a bartender and DJ at Mackie's. His personality fits right in. He's funny, sweet, and kindhearted. The rumor around town is that Keith and I are involved romantically behind closed doors. Every eye in the room is on us when we dance. They say we move in sync, gliding across the dance floor with grace. Regardless what they assume we are more like brother and sister. I can tell him my darkest secrets and count on him just like I can with Sara, but in a small town people make something out of nothing. I need to escape; a couple of drinks and laughter with good friends should do the trick. I tell Sara I will meet them at seven.

I have this way of hiding my emotions. I could be really upset but you would never have a clue unless you really knew me. I'm portrayed as unbreakable in everyone's eyes, but that's just because they can't see beneath the armor. The evening is going great and I've kept my emotions about Jace under cover until my phone rings. I hit ignore and turn off my phone.

"What are you doing? Wasn't that Jace?" asked Sara.

"You rejected Jace? Oh shit, Sara, hell's going to freeze over!" blurts Keith.

"Stop!" I snapped.

"What's wrong?" asked Sara.

"What did he do?" asked Keith.

They're not going to let me off the hook and the questions keep coming. I finally break.

"I haven't answered any of his calls today and I don't plan to. You can have his account!" I said to Sara.

Stirring my drink I'm fighting to hold back my tears when Keith hugs my neck.

"Talk to me baby girl, what's going on with you?" he asked.

"I'm in love with him and I have to stay away," I respond with tears in my eyes, "I never meant for this to happen, but it did, and now it's breaking my heart."

They both knew I was falling before I did! They really weren't shocked by my confession but you could see that my pain was their pain.

"Don't cry, Riley. You're making us cry," said Sara.

"We are here for you no matter what! You know that," said Keith.

We have a big group hug and Sara wipes my tears.

"Let's have one more round before we head home," I said.

I've already had one too many. I don't drink very often and everyone knows I don't handle alcohol well. Keith follows me home and makes sure I'm settled in. He lies next to me, consoling me, until I fall asleep.

My heart's restless and Jace rules my thoughts. I haven't answered his calls or text for three days. I'm hoping he gives up on me before I give in. My weakness for him is overwhelming. I have fallen hard. I throw myself into work to ease the void, going in early and staying late. Today's one of those days that I'm not even going home before I go on air. I'll just stay at the station and get an early start. I'm hoping the calls are steady throughout the night, which seems to help keep my mind from drifting off to Jace. The evening wares on and the more request that come in, the more I think there's a conspiracy to drive me insane! Every song requested plays on my emotions and takes me on a trip down memory lane. *I've had enough torture for one night.* I tell myself as I look at the hand on the clock slowly ticking. I announce the weather and sign off.

"Thank you for listening to the Wave. I'm Riley and I will see you tomorrow night at eight."

I gather my things and head out the door. The moon is full and lights up the parking lot like a football stadium. I lock the station door and turn around to head to my car. I look up and leaned against my car is Jace! I'm frozen in my tracks and speechless. He's not supposed to be back until this weekend and definitely not suppose to be here!

"What are you doing here?" I blurt out.

"I left early. I had to see you," he replied.

I walk pass him and put my things in the car.

"What are you doing?" he asks.

"What do you mean?" I replied, with this puzzled look on my face, "I was working."

"You know that's not what I'm talking about Riley! Why have you been ignoring my calls and texts?" he asked.

I'm dreading what I'm about to do, but I know I have to get it over with. I bow my head, with my heart breaking into a thousand pieces as I tell him we can no longer see each other. I won't look him in the eye because if I do, I will start to cry. I feel so nauseated from the despair of the words I just uttered.

"Why?" he asks, in panic.

"Because, I'm in love with you and you're married," I whisper, in defeat.

"Look at me, Riley!" he shouts. Taking his hand and lifting my head. "My wife and I live separate lives. We are strictly together to raise our daughter. We agreed to stay together for her sake and nothing more. I'm in love with you! Please don't do this."

The distraught look on his face and tears in his eyes told me he felt the same about me as I did him. It was in that moment I never looked back and Jace Carmichael became my world.

Chapter 5

The last eight months have been amazing. We spend every moment we can together. Jace's birthday is coming up, and I want to really make it special. I toss ideas around in my head all week when it hits me; I'll take him on a boxcar ride! I do it all the time when I want to clear my head. The train down from my house takes all the empty boxcars to Carson County and drops them off there until the next journey. I hop in one and ride to its destination and catch a bus back, or have Sara pick me up. I love the adventure it brings, and I feel like I'm leaving my worries behind. Roger, the train engineer knows I frequently catch a ride. He just smiles when he sees me get off. It's our little secret he says.

I call Sara to ask her to help with my plan. "I need your help to put my plan in motion for Jace's birthday," I said.

"What do you need?" she replies.

"I need you to follow me to Carson County to drop off my car and I will fill you in on the details on our way back."

I text Jace and tell him to pick me up at my house tomorrow evening at seven o'clock sharp. Sara and I discuss the arrangements and she agrees to set everything up that evening while I wait for Jace. I give her a list of the supplies and tell her to let her imagination run wild. We are both romantics and think alike so I know she will make me proud. Sara calls me through out the day to let me know how things are going.

"I will have everything set up and ready by seven. This is going to be amazing Riley! He will never experience anything like this again!" she exclaims.

A million and one things go running through my mind while I'm waiting on Jace. *Will he think I'm crazy? What if he refuses to go once I get him there?* I've gotten myself all worked up with worry by the time he arrives. I'm nervous as ever, but I take a deep breath and put the wheels in motion. I walk out to the truck and tell him to get in the passenger side and let me drive.

"Where are we going?" he asks.

"You ask too many questions," I reply.

He walks around to the passenger side and I hand him a blindfold saying, "Put this on."

"I'm scared to!" he replied.

I help him put it on and make sure he can't peek before I get in the driver's seat.

I park the truck at a dead end road, by the tracks, where Sara and Keith will come to pick it up. We walk down the tracks and the curiosity is killing him.

"Where are we? Where is that music coming from? When can I take this off?" he asks.

"We're almost there," I reply, "be patient!"

We get to the boxcar and I remove his blindfold.

"Happy Birthday!" I shout.

"Why is there music coming from a boxcar, and why are we here?" he asks.

The expression on his face is a mixture of curiosity and confusion rolled into one.

"We're going for a ride!" I reply.

"Riley, we can't just hop on a train. We could get in a lot of trouble if we get caught," he said.

I laugh and state, "I have this under control. I arranged it with my friend Roger, the engineer, trust me its ok."

I slide open the door and have Jace help me inside. I take his hand and help him up. He looks around in shock. There are lanterns casting a dim glow around a pile of pillows and blankets. In the corner, there is a CD player filling the air with ballads from some of the greatest love songs ever written. There is a bottle of wine chilling on ice and a bowl of fruit sitting on top of a crate covered in white lining. I leave the door open so we can watch the sunset paint the sky and feel the gentle breeze that fills the evening air. The train is getting ready to depart and you can feel the tugging and shifting of the boxcar.

"You might want to sit down until we get going," I said.

Jace comes and sits next to me in the door of the car. The sun is setting and the sky is exploding with vibrate colors.

"I don't know what to say Riley. I'm speechless. No one has ever done something like this for me," he said.

The ride has now become slow and steady, so I get up and pour us both a glass of wine. "Thank you for boarding the night train, it's designed for your escape. Let the fairytale begin," I said with a smile. We drank our wine, talked about life, and gazed at the stars.

We shared laughter and intimacy as we allowed each other to drift into uncharted waters closed off to the outside world. The song that started to play is one of my favorite ballads. I grab Jace by the hand, "Dance with me!" I said.

"I can't dance. I never learned how!" he exclaims.

"I will teach you," I reply, as I place his hands on my hips and I wrap my arms around his neck.

"Close your eyes and feel the music," I whisper.

He places his head against mine and we close our eyes getting lost in the lyrics.

"You show me a world I've never known Riley! It's pure and simple, yet magical all in one," he whispered softly.

He takes my hand and leads me over to the blanket pulling me down gently. He puts one hand behind my head and lays me back kissing my neck softly. His breath on my skin causes my body to tremble. The taste of his kiss is that of strawberry wine, leaving me drunk and thirsting for more.

"Breathe Riley", he whispers, as he unbuttons my blouse.

Our bodies glisten from the intensity of heat and passion. He takes a piece of ice from the bucket and begins to trace my body as if it were a wonderland. Starting with my lips, he works his way down.

He has one hand in mine, and I have one hand tangled in his hair, as if I was guiding his movement. Quenching his thirst, he used his tongue to lavish each drop as it rolls down my body. The silhouette of his frame above mine was breathtaking. The ripples across his stomach and bulging biceps showed great strength yet he cradled me with utter tenderness. We are overwhelmed with passion and desire. There's magic in his fingertips that electrify my senses. This is a conversation between his heart and mine, yet no words are spoken. Our pulses are racing as we lie together with our bodies entwined. Gently he thrusts his hips against mine and in perfect rhythm we slowly grind. The air is filled with whimpers and moans from the pleasure we can no longer contain. The love that surrounds us can not be denied as two souls became one for the first time. We soar to ecstasy and then collapse into each other's arms; physically and emotionally drained. The feelings I get when we're together are different than anything I've ever known. It's more than just an attraction between us. We've awakened something inside that leaves us both visibly shaken to the core.

The morning dawn is creeping up and our journey is near its end as the whistle blows to signal our arrival. We gather our things and load them in the car. The drive home is bittersweet as reality sinks in.

"What are your plans for the rest of the weekend?" he asked.

"I plan on helping at the soup kitchen and then doing yard work, other than that not much," I reply.

"You feed homeless people? You shouldn't be doing that or mowing your yard!"

The demeanor in his voice caught me off guard.

"What do you mean by that?" I replied.

"Riley, you're too good for that!" he says. "Let someone else serve soup. You don't know what those crazy people might do."

"I can't believe you!" I snarled. "That's what's wrong with the world, people like you! Those people are just as equal as you and I. They have names and bleed just like you!" I said in haste. "Jace, money doesn't make you special or buy love and happiness. The greatest feeling in the world is helping someone down on their luck or bringing a smile to a broken heart. The faster you learn that the better off you'll be."

"You're crazy Riley!" he said with a smirk.

"Maybe I am, but you should try it sometime," I said.

"I was right, you're an angel Riley. I have my very own saving grace, but Ill tell you now, I'm not doing all that super hero stuff," he said, laughing uncontrollably.

"That's fine some people just don't have what it takes to be a hero!"

He gets me all riled up only to make me burst into laughter. We can never make each other mad for long. I get up Sunday and meet Keith at the soup kitchen at ten thirty. This is our little tradition we do together and it's something we both enjoy.

"Good morning sunshine!" he hollers across the parking lot.

"Hello rainbow!" I said laughing. "I see you survived your night out with Mr. High class."

"Do I detect some jealousy in your voice?" I ask.

"I'll say this, it would not have hurt my feelings if he would have fell of the train," he stated.

I shove him ahead of me, "That was mean Keith, be nice! I can't believe you said that!"

Laughing he said, "I don't care where you are or who you're with you will always be my girl. I don't like his demeanor he thinks he's better than everybody is and that gets under my skin."

"I have to admit, he does come across antisocial but once you get to know him you can see there's something special about him. Stop judging a book by its cover," I said.

I must have hit a nerve.

"You know I like to pick on you Riley," he said laughing.

The time flies and Keith walks me to my car.

"I will see you and Sara Tuesday night. Be careful going home," he says, as he leans in the window.

He kisses my cheek and watches as I drive away. I pull into the driveway and stop my car. I can not believe what I'm seeing! I watch intently as Jace circles around the yard on a riding mower. This is a man that pays people to mow his yard and thinks he's too good for physical labor, let alone getting all sweaty and dirty. I pull up and get out trying not to look too impressed. I go in the house and pour a glass of sweet tea and bring it to him.

"What is this?" I exclaim.

"I was told charity work was good for the soul, so I thought I would give it a try," he said with sarcasm. "What?" I say, "I'm not a charity case! I'm perfectly capable of mowing my own yard!"

He takes a big gulp of his tea and then said, "I'm trying to see things your way. Go sit down and enjoy the view!"

I can't help but laugh.

"Carry on," I say, as I walk away.

The view is delightful as his body glistens from the heat of the summer sun. I sit on the porch and think to myself there is so much more about this man than he allows the world to see. I don't know why I'm the lucky one to experience it but I'm honored. He makes his last round and pulls up to his truck and loads his things. I watch and wait patiently for him to finish, assuming he will visit with me and finish his tea before he leaves but he stops at the bottom of the stairs. He props one leg behind him and leans against porch. He wipes the sweat from his brow and stares straight ahead. He never even glanced my way before blurting out, "You were right!"

"About what?" I ask. "All that stuff about helping others, money doesn't buy love or happiness, and it's the simple things blah, blah, blah!"

I sit in silence for a minute and then reply, "My cup runith over!"

He turns and walks to his truck leaving me sitting there to ponder this moment. The beauty of our relationship is we can read each other's thoughts and silence has never said so much! He is learning what love really is and I'm learning that it does exist.

I watch as he leaves and the smile on my face lingers. I know in some twist of faith that our worlds have collided for a reason. I'm sitting there but my mind is a million miles away in solitude when a message comes across my cell. It was simple but spoke volumes:

You make me want to be a better man.

I instantly text back.

You give me purpose.

The bond between us is unique and powerful. It's one that I don't fully understand and can't explain myself but it exceeds what we are taught love should be.

Chapter 6

I have always put what I feel into words. Writing is a form of release for me. I keep them in a binder safely tucked away. No one even knows they exist except for Sara and a few other close friends. Most of them are my theories about life; how devastation has been a friend of mine. I've had more than my share of tragedies and carry a lot of scars. My childhood was far from normal. By the tender age of nine, I had already known abandonment, abuse, and rape. I have been on my own since I was fourteen years old. Having no one in life to turn to. Sara says she doesn't see how I have overcome the hand life has dealt me, let alone be so kind hearted. I don't dwell on it and I know in my heart there is something more.

Since I have met Jace the love and happiness has out written the sad. He shines light into the darkness I was accustomed to. He makes me feel alive. I always read to him during our late night conversations and he encourages me to do something with them instead of letting them collect dust. He sends me a link to enter a poetry contest with a caption that reads:

'Riley, do this for yourself if not, then do it for me. You have a gift that should be shared with the world.'

I give little thought to his suggestion at first, but tell him I will think about it.

"Stop thinking Riley, and do it," he replies, "It's late close your eyes and rest that beautiful mind. I'll call you tomorrow."

I let the thought of entering the contest dance around in my head all night. The next morning I decide to review the contestant rules. Sara comes in the office as I'm going over the details.

"What's this?" she asked, leaning over my shoulder.

"Nothing!" I click off the screen.

"Are you going to enter? You should!" she states.

"It's hard for me to share my poetry Sara," I plead, "When people read what I write it's like they have the opportunity to see inside my soul."

"Why does that scare you so much Riley?" she asks.

"I guess because everyone sees me as this tough-as-nails individual that can't be broken. When in reality there are so many scars, my heart weeps. People take advantage of kindness and tenderness Sara. They twist you, use you, and play on your emotions until there's nothing left." I pause before adding, "Then they leave you tainted and broken. I guess what I'm trying to say is I don't want to be a cold, heartless person. My heart is fragile already. It's like a fine piece of crystal. The more people who handle it the better chance there is that it will get broken."

"That's too deep for me, but that's why I love you," said Sara, "but I'm with Jace on this one, you are cheating the world of something beautiful."

"Ok! I'll do it but I'm leaving it up to you to pick the one I submit!" I said in amusement.

"I'll come over after work and bring the wine and tissue," she said smiling.

Sara gets to the house around eight-thirty and we read over hundreds of poems. We read, talk, laugh, cry and read some more; until Sara comes across a recent one I had written for Jace.

"This is it! Submit this one, it is perfect!" she states.

As she begins to read it a loud.

> *Is it wise to put your heart on the line?*
> *Risk everything you have for one moment in time?*
>
> *When you know from the start, at some point it ends.*
> *Leavening you only to wish for that moment again.*
>
> *My heart surrenders and I must confess.*
> *I would give anything, I would give my last breath!*
>
> *Just to hold you for a little while,*
> *to hear your voice and see you smile.*
>
> *To hear your heartbeat and taste your lips,*
> *to touch your body with my fingertips.*
>
> *If for only an hour between your heart and mine,*
> *I would risk everything for that moment in time!*

"Riley, I wish I could have just a taste of the love that you and Jase share," Sara says. "It's like a fairytale that every girl dreams of. Except I watch you live it every day."

I hit the submit button and tell Sara it's all done.

"When will you know something?" she replies.

"I'm not sure. In the overview it said they would contact me by mail. I guess for now we just wait!" I say.

I don't tell Jase right away that I entered the contest because I don't want to let him down if I don't place. He inquires during our phone conversation and I fill him in on the details. A couple of weeks have gone by and I have given up on checking the mail everyday. Sara inquires everyday and tries to keep my hope alive. I'm just thinking how ashamed I am that I've let her down. I'm a little bummed out but decide I'll check the mail anyway. I flip through, separating bills from ads and in the middle there was a letter from *The Poets Society*. I stare at it terrified of what it might say. I sit it on the table. I have to build up the courage to open it and was stunned by what I was reading:

> *Ms. Davis this letter is to congratulate you on ranking in the top ten. Your poem was chosen out of the hundreds received. Here is your personal invitation to receive your award at the Poets Convention in Washington DC.*

I immediately call Sara.

"I told you!" she shouted, "When do you leave? We need to go shopping!" she stated.

"I'm not going," I replied.

"What! Why?" she asked.

You can hear the excitement leave her voice.

"I can't afford to fly to Washington and stay for a week Sara, I just can't!" I answer.

"We can figure this out and make it work Riley. I will help and maybe Jase will to!" she replies.

"Absolutely not Sara!" I exclaim.

"Are you even going to tell him?" she asked.

"I will just avoid the conversation if he brings it up and tell him I haven't heard anything," I said.

"I hate the fact that you're not able to go, Riley, it makes me sad," says Sara.

"I'm ok knowing that I qualified, let alone that I placed in the top ten Sara. That's better than I thought I would do! We can celebrate together one night this week at Mackie's."

The next day I have to go to see Jace at his office to renew his contract. I know he is going to ask me about the contest and I'm not going to be able to lie. I'm no good at it first off and secondly he can read me like a book. I decide to tell him I placed in the top fifty or so but leave out the trip to Washington. I get to the counter and chat with Katie for a moment before she informs Jace of my arrival.

"He's ready for you Riley," Katie said with a smile.

"It was good seeing you," I reply as I head down the hall.

I think Katie has her suspicions about Jace and me but if she does, she keeps it to herself. We go over the contract and talk about our day, "Have you heard anything on the contest yet?" he asked.

"I received a conformation letter yesterday," I reply.

"Well how did you do?" he asks.

"They chose the top fifty and I was somewhere in there. I don't really remember," I said.

"This calls for celebration! What are your plans for this evening?" he asked.

Now I'm in a pickle. I tell myself.

"Well Sara and Keith invited me to Mackie's for dinner and I already accepted, but you're welcome to join us."

I really expect him to decline the offer when he blurts out, "What time shall I be there?"

I stumble on my reply.

"Seven-thirty."

He laughs, "I will pick you up at seven!"

We get to Mackie's and I pull Sara to the side while we wait on Keith to arrive.

"I haven't told him anything about the trip or that I made it to the top ten. So let's keep the conversation to a minimal."

Sara agrees and we join Jace at the table. Keith arrives and Jace orders a bottle of wine.

"I want to make a toast to a beautiful mind," said Jace.

"A talented one to make it to the top ten out of hundreds and win an award," blurted Keith.

I almost dropped my glass. The look on Sara's face and mine was total disarray!

"Isn't she amazing? How could you forget to tell me that Riley?" asks Jase in an alarming tone.

I feel bad for lying and at the same time want to throw Keith over the rail into the Bayou.

"It's really not a big deal and the award is a certificate," I said.

"I'm sure it is," said Jace in a sarcastic tone.

Sara hasn't spoken a word as she steadily keeps drinking the wine. She knows she can't save me now and she doesn't want to make things worse. The rest of the evening is awkward at best but we still manage to have some fun and laughter. The next couple of days Jace is still upset with me for lying and gives me a hard time. He seems to throw "somewhere in the top fifty" out every chance he gets. I deserve the sly remarks and understand why he's upset.

It's late Friday afternoon when I pull up my e-mail and see a message from Carmichael's Construction. I open it immediately wondering why he emailed instead of calling. The e-mail is conformation for a round trip flight to Washington DC, hotel reservations for a week at the Hilton, and a message that read:

> Riley,
>   *Your writing is a gift share it with the world because of you I want to know what love is! I'm so proud of you.*
>   Jace

I can't help but wonder if he has a clue that he is the inspiration to my madness. The poetry I write is about my love for him. He deserves the award for bringing such depth to my emotion. He brings something alive inside me. Before he came I was just an empty shell trying to find hope in a dark, cold world.

Chapter 7

I never really questioned Jace much on his marriage. We discussed it on occasion. It always came down to Jace putting his daughter first and staying until she graduated. He told me of the struggle he went through when his parents divorce and how he felt pulled between the two.

"You go from being a happy carefree child, to an object used for leverage to punish the other parent," he said.

He promised himself he would never do that to his child. I, being one to never have had a stable home or stable parents for that matter, could grasp his reasons and completely relate. That only made me admire him more. I could never make him choose. Or was I afraid I would loose him if I did? I still had my moments of fighting myself between what I was doing, and what was right. I couldn't help but believe that we where made for each other, or then again, was that what I wanted it to be?

Months turned into years and I dreamed of the day I would be his forever. We acted like a married couple, did things like a married couple, and spent almost all our time together. We just couldn't confess our love to the world.

"Mark it down Riley Davis, your day is coming when we will wake up next to each other everyday and shout from the rooftops of the love we found in each other," he would say.

I believed in my heart that day would come but for now was grateful for what I had. We never lost the magic in our relationship everything was like the first time not only for me but Jace felt it to. He was just excited to hear my voice as I was his, and we couldn't wait to be near each other. We where making love while the world around us disappeared. He called me his Angel, his saving grace, but in reality he was mine. Over the years Jace has changed his outlook on life and started to see things my way, as he gracefully puts it. We have taught each other so much and changed each other for the better. He now serves soup, gives donations, and even goes to church. He helps me with furnishing clothing for the shelters and even has great ideas of his own. I have been restored with hope, dreams, love and faith.

I have been spending Tuesday's and Wednesday's at the Cabin and driving back and fourth to work. Jace also spends a few nights at my house during the week. Sara and Keith take turns watching my place while I'm away.

"Wednesday is your anniversary, isn't it?" asked Sara. "How many years has it been?"

I smile, "Six years Sara, and it has been the best years of my life!"

"You can see the love between you two and I want a love like that," said Sara. "I've never seen two people give themselves so completely to each other and grow as one. It's what you dream of finding only it never happens. I can say this though, I thought I knew what love was and how it should be, but realized I haven't even come close now that I've witnessed yours and Jase!"

Sara helps me pack my things and sees me off. I get to the Cabin late because I had to record my shift at the station for both nights. The pier is lit up like runway lights. I can see the silhouette of Jase sitting at its edge. Jace greets me with a glass of wine.

"I have a surprise for you," he said, as he kissed my cheek.

He walks me to the end of the pier and drifting in the still of the night, is a raft. Built of logs, piled with blankets, and surrounded by lanterns.

"After you," he motions, as he helps me aboard.

He ties the raft to the dock but allows enough rope for us to drift a few hundred feet away in the bayou. The soft glow of the lanterns danced across the water giving way to the moonlight. The waves swayed the raft back and forth rocking us gently. The crickets sung us a slumbering lullaby.

Wrapped in his arms I had my very own heaven here on earth. The peace and tranquility of our surroundings has set the stage for a conversation of the hearts.

"I'm not good at expressing my emotions like you," he whispered. "I wish I could put into words how you make me feel. The love I have for you, Riley."

"Have you ever tried to write it down?" I asked.

"I go blank," he said, with a smile.

"Well, what if I wanted you to do that for me instead of buying me gifts?" I replied.

"It's not going to happen," he said. "So don't expect it."

He pulls me tight.

"Close your eyes and get lost with me."

"You don't have to say anything," I whisper, "I can feel your love."

We keep our love behind closed doors, a secret from the world, to protect the innocent from the storm. Our love is like a hurricane. The eye of a hurricane is peaceful and beautiful, that's Jase and I together. The secrets that we keep are swirling around us. This is the part of the hurricane that causes devastation and destruction. I truly believe one day we will take this wrong and make it right, but for now, we wait. I always say there is a season for everything. Time and reason under the heavens. Jace still makes fun of my philosophies and we still butt heads with our attitudes. This is the beauty of our relationship. We try to see it from the others perspective and gracefully agree to disagree. We are grateful for the small things and thrive in the aura that surrounds each other. Our time together always seems to fly by. I'm always filled with dread when it's time to leave.

The two days apart seems like a million years but our phone conversations carry me through. The sound of his voice calms my raging sea. I get back in the stream of work so, Sara and Keith fill the void. Keith stops by to drop off my mail.

"I missed you sassy," he says, as he gives me a big hug.

"I missed you to. Thank you for taking care of things," I reply.

"Sara and I took turns, but I gathered all your mail. Let me say, that man is weird, sending you letters while your with him!" he said, laughing.

"What?" I say, as I grab the mail.

There it was, with no return address, just *Jase* written across the top. I set the letter aside.

"Amazing!"

Keith looks at me with this puzzled look.

"More like weird!" he said.

"I don't know how, or when he could have done this. I will tell you this though Keith. I want to stay lost inside his weirdness."

"Well I'm gonna let you drown in it!" he said, laughing. "At least until you tell me other wise, but I have a life vest waiting with your name on it."

He hugs me tight and kisses my cheek.

"If anyone deserves to be happy Riley, it would be you." he says.

"Stop! Before you make me cry," I whisper. "I love you big Keith!"

"I will see you tomorrow, get some rest!" he said.

I walk him to the door and thank him again.

I prepare myself to read my letter by gathering a few things I know I will need, some tissues to collect my emotions, and something to drink, to wash down this lump in my throat. I get situated and comfortable then break the seal. My hands are trembling and my heart is pounding. It doesn't matter if it's a few lines or six pages. Words that are written hold a greater measure than any words spoken. I guess that's the belief of a poet anyway. Anything we put on paper comes from our hearts.

I unfold the page and instantly smile. It's hand written on company Letterhead from his office. I admire the logo *Curmichael's Construction* written in big bold blue letters. The cursive script laid out before me grabs my attention. My mind paints a picture of Jace as I read a loud.

> *My Love,*
> *I am writing this as I watch you sleep and I want you to know you are everything to me. My life would not be complete without you. You have taught me things I never knew existed. I can say true love and compassion are your mainstay. Your philosophies and you have many of them! I myself have come to believe in and live by. You are the most unselfish and loving person I have ever met. You are everything the human spirit should be. You're beautiful, intelligent, gentle and kind yet so humble. You're the perfect earth angle! You told me once that your goal in life was to leave an impression on something or someone, well you can say mission accomplished! Your name is forever carved in my heart. You have taught me what love is and you where right, the simple things are the best. I want you to know that I love you and I need you in my life. You are my soul mate and saving grace. I love and admire you Riley Davis, never forget that!*
>
> *Jace*

I don't think he understands the gift he has given me. It's not just the words. The thought, time, and effort he has put in to this letter, which makes it a prize possession to me. I can see myself, pulling this out of the hope chest, in twenty years. Reading it to him as our youth has dwindled, giving way to time, but our love has not.

Chapter 8

The time has slipped away so fast through the years. I don't even find our relationship out of the ordinary. It's hard to believe that we have been together this long. It still seems as though it was yesterday that we where defying each other. I would have never thought from our first encounter that we would be friends. Let alone that he would become the love of my life. My world is complete. I have my two best friends, who would do anything for me, and Jace, who makes me whole. The cruelty and devastation of life as I knew it has been wiped away and restored with faith hope and love.

I'm sitting around the house bored out of my mind when Sara shows up.

"Go get dressed!" she hollers from the driveway. "Tonight is girl's night and we are going to the casino."

"You could not have showed up at a better time," I squeal, "come inside while I get ready. I was looking for something to do you must have read my mind."

"Great minds think alike! What's Jace doing tonight?" ask Sara.

"I'm not sure he hasn't called yet and I can't call him because he's at home," I reply.

"That has to be hard Riley not being able to call him and having to wait until he calls you," Sara says. "That would drive me insane!"

"It bothers me sometimes but it's become normal it's been this way for so long," I sigh. "It worries me sometimes that if something where to happen to either one of us we wouldn't find out until the next day. Jace has never failed to call and tell me goodnight. He always gets on to me about stuff like that. His theory is that I'm so use to bad things happening that I've grown accustoms to it. I need to try not to worry so much."

"Well I would be just like you Riley, he must not see that black cloud that follows you around," Sara said laughing.

"Thanks a lot!" I reply.

"I'm just stating a fact," said Sara. "If it can happen, it happens to you Riley Davis!"

"It looks as though my luck has changed I have you, Jace and Keith. I couldn't be happier or ask for more!" I stated with a smile from ear to ear. "I can tell you this Sara I live for every moment I have with him. In a couple more years my wait will be worth while. I will wake up to him every morning and close my eyes tangled up in his arms every night. I love everything about him including his arrogant attitude," I said.

"I will be so happy for you Riley and if he loves you half as much as you do him it will be a fairytale come true. I'm jealous of what you two have and hope one day I find someone that can make me complete," said Sara.

We get inside and start playing the slots that's our favorite. Neither Sara nor I have any interest in the table games. The night drags on and I'm not having any luck at all. Sara comes and sits next to me and after a couple spins she hits the sizzling sevens. She screams at the top of her lungs and I am in total disbelief.

"I have been feeding this machine all night and you sit down and hit on twenty dollars!" I exclaim.

"It's that black cloud hovering over you," she stated, laughing. "I will treat you to dinner."

"I'm glad you won Sara. I want steak," I said as we bust into laughter.

Sara collects her winnings and we decide to head home before I go broke.

"Come on let's go have dinner, my treat!" she said.

She drives up to Rosendales. It's one of the high-end steak houses in the area. A place neither one of us could afford unless we were having crackers and water.

"Let's eat!" she screeched.

"Are you serious Sara?" I reply.

"Look Riley we may never get the chance to come here again. Tonight we do, thanks to the sizzling sevens," Sara said.

The second we walk inside all eyes are on us! Everyone is dressed in business attire, and here we are, in jeans and a tee shirt. We are not ashamed and proudly walk with our waiter to our seats. This place is a very elegant with the white lining draped over the tables and chandeliers hanging like teardrops. The wall behind us is made of glass filled with delicate wines. The atmosphere is pleasing with the soft glow of candlelit dancing across the tables and the sound of classical music filling the air. We glance over the menu, astonished at the prices of things we cannot even pronounce.

"What will you be having?" Sara asked.

"That all depends on how much water and breadcrumbs are," I said laughing.

"Boy! We sure make the odd couple here," said Sara.

"Yes we do, so this means you must be on your best behavior Sara. Meaning you can not draw more attention by licking your spoon," I said.

"This is Jace's kind of life style, you better get use to it Riley!" said Sara.

I start laughing as I say, "I could enjoy this every now and then, for special occasions, but I'm more for having a glass of wine and grilling. I made his favorite last week fried pork chops and this weekend he is cooking me Gumbo! I will save sum and we can eat it for lunch."

"Well that doesn't surprise me! This man is right out of the pages of a famous romance novel according to you," said Sara.

"I must confess I'm the lucky one!" I replied.

We enjoyed our evening and head home when I noticed I had a text from Jace. His daughters dance recital was tonight and he was running late.

I'm sorry I didn't get to call you, I stopped by to see you but you weren't home. I will call you in the morning.

I get home and on the porch are a dozen roses and a movie, by my favorite author, that I had been dying to see. Attached was a note that read:

I wanted to see what all the fuss was about so I figured we could watch this together this weekend.

It's times like this that it bothers me and reminds me of the secrets that we keep. I can't reply back to his text or call and thank him. Sometimes it makes me really sad and reality slaps me across the face. Reminding me of how wrong I am morally. It's an on going battle that rages inside me, but the thought of giving Jace up, is more than I can fathom. I can only hope and pray that God will forgive me, and in the end, we will right this wrong. I pray for forgiveness every night when I say my prayers. I also thank him for putting Jace in my life. I have to believe that he knows that my heart desires to do right. Even though my love for Jace overrides and wins the battle that pulls on me like a game of tug of war. The world could never understand how difficult this situation is, unless they have walked a mile in my shoes. It seems unfair that I should even be tested in such a manor. That I would have to give up the one thing that makes my heart beat, the very air I breath, in order to be morally correct. How or why would our two worlds collide, allowing two souls to become one, if it wasn't meant to be? The struggle to understand is beyond any comprehension of the human spirit. So for now I continue to justify in my own mind, what my heart desires.

Chapter 9

Christmas is my favorite time of the year. I love the magic in the air, and the excitement on the faces of children. I'm not one to want or have a wish list. I like to be the one to make wishes come true and put a smile on someone's face. I love to adopt names off of the local Christmas tree. Children who are in shelters or families that have fallen on hard times and being the one to brighten their world. It's all done anonymously and that's my favorite part. Giving is the best gift you can give yourself that's always been my motto. I pick one girl and one boy and sometimes I do two of each, all depending on what my bonus check from work looks like. Jace and I have made it a tradition over the last few years to do it together. He basically furnishes some of the money and occasionally helps me wrap the gifts, but he doesn't do the shopping. He leaves that part to me.

Our holidays are a little altered for the situation; Jace spends a couple hours with me on Christmas Eve and then spends Christmas with his family. We usually celebrate the day after together and have our own private celebration. I always buy him a few gifts but I like to make something that money cant buy. This year I have taken all my poetry that I have written about him, over the last ten years, and made him a book. I believe home made gifts are the best. It's so easy to go buy something, but to put thought into something and make it original. Means it truly comes from the heart being made with love. I have been working on this for two months and I'm excited to give it to him. We have made plans to spend Sunday together being he will leave Monday to go out of town for work. I can hardly contain my excitement of his arrival. I live for these moments we share.

It's around ten thirty when I hear him drive up. I run to the door to greet him, leaping into his arms, causing him drop the bag he was carrying. I wrap my arms around his neck, the smile on my face is from ear to ear.

"Did you miss me?" he asked.

"Not really!" I reply.

"Oh! So you always greet people by throwing yourself at them?" he smirks.

"Maybe," I said still smiling. He put me down and kisses my cheek.

"Help me get this inside," he said, handing me a bag.

"Are these for me?" I ask inquisitively.

"No! I brought them for me!" he said with sarcasm.

He takes them out of the bags and puts them under the tree next to his.

"Someone is spoiled!" he said, as he stacks the gifts up, leaving no space under the tree.

We start preparing to cook our Christmas dinner together. Jace puts on some music and I get out a bottle of our favorite wine. I prepare the trimmings while Jace tackles the ham. In the process of making the desert, we end up in a battle that leads to flour all over the place. He chases me around the island before catching me and pinning me against the counter. Giggles and laughter fill the air. He brushes my hair from my face to gently kiss my lips.

"I love you Jace Carmichael, with all my soul," I whisper, holding him tight.

"I love you to Riley," he replies, as he caresses my hair.

The evening is perfect! The lights are down low and the soft glow of the candles ads charm to the twinkling lights from the Christmas tree. We indulge with delight in our meal that we prepared together before we open our gifts. The music is turned down low and inviting. I grab him by the hand and we dance.

"I want this night to last forever and I wish we could be together everyday," I say.

He looks me in the eye and replies, "Wishes do come true and this is your year Riley! You are what I want for the rest of my life and I'm going to file for divorce after the first of the year!"

I swear my heart stopped beating. I could not believe what I was hearing. I have waited for an eternity to hear those words. I am so overwhelmed with emotion I cant utter a word but the tears that stream down my face says it all.

He scoops me in his arms and carries me to the bedroom. Falling back he cradles my head in his hand. No words are spoken; we are reading each other's minds. Our union is telepathic and our bodies answer the yearning desire from deep within. His eyes tell me that this moment will forever be imprinted in our hearts. The love in the air drapes our bodies like a blanket. Each movement is played in slow motion. When he touches me, it's as if he's caressing my soul. My mind is capturing every detail, from the smell of his cologne, to the look in his eyes. Our hearts beat in one rhythm and our bodies answer to the desire of the other. Like the still of a photograph, my memory is storing every detail. From our movements, to the silhouette of our bodies entwined as one. Every emotion of passion and desire that weeps from our pores is soaked in to my soul. This is beyond human comprehension, we are in the spiritual realm and it's earth shaking. We are two entities merging as one: divulging in uncharted territory. We have far exceeded the realm of making love and are on the verge of what could be considered as a heavenly divine. I don't think we will ever experience the magnitude of this union. I'm not even sure its possible. I do know the merging of two hearts is complete as one. I fall asleep to his breath on my skin cradled in his arms.

The sound of the alarm came way to quickly. I wanted nothing more but to stay wrapped in his heaven. I jump up, trying not to wake him, and head down stairs to make him breakfast. I want to surprise him before he leaves to go out of town for a couple days. I make his favorite: two eggs, over easy, grits, bacon and toast.

"Wake up sunshine!" I blurted, as I walked into the room.

"What's this?" he asked, as he rubs the sleep from his eyes.

"Breakfast for champions!" I exclaim.

"You are my hero Riley Davis," he mutters.

"And you are my Kryptonite!" I gasp.

I help him pack his things.

"How long will you be gone?" I ask.

"Two days. I'll be back with you on Wednesday," he said kissing my forehead.

He heads out the door to his truck when I yell, "Come back, I forgot something!"

I can tell he's in a hurry but he graciously walks toward me.

"What is it? I have to go," he said with haste.

"I wanted to give you this and forgot to tell you, I love you!" I say, as I hand him a CD.

"It's a song that describes what it's like when you really love someone. This is how I feel about you! I love you," I whispered.

"You are so deep Riley. I love you too! You know that," he said.

"Well you never know! What if something happened and we never told each other how we felt. There's no promise for tomorrow," I said smiling.

He kisses me and shakes his head.

"You're a mess girl, stop thinking crazy!" he replies. "I will call you tonight and I will be back before you know it."

"I'll be right here waiting," I reply.

I watch him drive away until I could no longer see the taillights.

Three thirty was way to early and I have a couple hours to sleep before I need to be up for work. I head up stairs and snuggle the pillow covered with the sent of his cologne. I get to the office and text Jace to make sure he made it ok. He sends me a reply telling me he made it and will call me later. Sara pops in from around the corner.

"Let's have it. What did you get? How was your weekcnd?"

I'm beaming with excitement and can't hold it back. I tell Sara what Jace had told me; my wait is over that I would be waking up in his arms everyday for the rest of my life!

"Oh my God! I am so happy for you Riley! If two people belong together it would be you and Jace. I still find it hard to believe it's been ten years ago that you had your first meeting. I will never forget how you described the first encounter; it's funny how time flies," she says smiling.

That evening Jace calls and tells me he is not feeling well. He said that around lunchtime he started feeling like he had the flu.

"I'm going to take some cold medication and get some rest my whole body aches," he explains. "I will call you tomorrow. Sweet dreams and I love you!"

"I wish I were there to take care of you I love you more," I replied.

Chapter 10

I wake up Tuesday morning at my usual time. I call Jace first thing to check on him. The phone rings three times and then goes to voice mail. I leave him a message and ask him to text or call me. It's mid day and I still have had no response from Jace so I call him again. I get his voice mail and leave a hasty message; *I know your busy but I'm worried and the least you could do is text me damn it Jace call me back!* By the time I start my radio shift I still have not heard a word from Jace and I am livid! I'm a mixture of worried and aggravated. I call Sara rambling about how when he does call, he's got a few choice words coming! She tries to calm me down by telling me there has to be a reasonable explanation.

"Maybe he lost his phone or it got wet and it's not working?" she said.

"I guess your right that would explain it," I answer. "I don't know Sara, I just have a bad feeling. He has never not called or text me ever!"

The nights are unkind, as I toss and turn with a million things running through my mind. Thursday morning I drag myself to the office and close the door. The bags under my eyes tell the story of sleepless nights and endless tears. I have no way of knowing what's going on. I'm left in the dark with a million questions. Sara comes in as I burst into tears.

"He didn't show up and I still haven't heard from him!" I said burying my head in my hands.

"I'm so sorry Riley. Maybe he changed his mind and just don't know how to tell you," she said.

"No Sara!" I shout. "He would call and tell me. We talk about everything. He wouldn't walk away without saying goodbye! He wouldn't do that to me Sara!"

"Have you tried calling his office?" she asks.

"I have and it goes to his voice mail. I don't know what else to do," I said sobbing uncontrollably.

"We will figure this out together! Let's get you back home, you can't work like this," said Sara.

She drives me home and walks me inside. I lay on the couch staring in silence and watch the clock tic.

"I'm so confused and I don't understand," I whisper.

Sara covers me with a blanket saying, "Riley, get some rest and when I get back we will call his secretary. We will see what information we can get out of her. I won't be gone long, I promise!"

I'm laying there staring into space and the thoughts in my mind are going a million mile per second. *He would call me even if he had changed his mind! I have no doubt but what could be stopping him?* I want to believe there is a good explanation and my craziness is foolish but my heart tells me otherwise. I'm a ten-year secret that no one knows about except for Sara and Keith. I have no one to talk to and no way to find out any information. I'm none existent in his world. Hours pass when Sara returns and we try to think of ways to find out if he's ok.

"Let's take a drive and see if his truck is at work! On the way, you can decide on some choice words for when you see him," she said smiling.

"If he's there, I have nothing to say, that just tells me I never meant anything!" I say with anger in my voice.

That hour drive was the longest drive of my life. The unknowing of the situation was a scary place to be. We drive into the parking lot of Carmichael's Construction and it looks like a ghost town. There is not a car to be seen; the business should not be closed for two more hours. I am on pins and needles and completely beside myself. Sara gets out and goes to the door. I stand beside the car watching and praying someone's still inside.

Sara bows her head as she turns in my direction. You can feel the dread looming in the air.

"It's locked Riley! I'm so sorry," she said.

I don't even reply defeat shows on my face as I turn to open the car door. I start to get inside when a car comes from around the back of the building.

"I wonder who that is?" asked Sara.

"I have no idea, but they are heading in our direction," I reply.

Sara and I are standing there when Kayla gets out of the car.

"Hello Riley! What are you doing here?" she asked.

She had a puzzled look on her face. Immediately Sara takes over the conversation.

"Riley and I came to talk with Mr. Carmichael about some advertising. We didn't realize you would be closing this early. What's the occasion?" Sara asked.

Kayla's face goes blank and she replies, "Oh gosh you haven't heard?"

"Heard what?" I blurt.

"Riley, Jase is really sick and they don't know what's wrong. They found him unresponsive Tuesday at his hotel. The last report I got was they don't expect him to live!"

My knees are weak so I grab on to the car. I can't register what I just heard.

"There has to be a mistake!" I say to myself.

I'm in total disbelief of what's happening. Shock and fear has left me paralyzed and unable to respond or utter a word. The look of confusion and disorientation on my face told the story of shock and despair. Sara takes over the conversation cutting it short before I completely lose control. My body is reacting and everything is going haywire. The beating of my heart is faint. I can barely breath; the air is thick and I can't get enough in. My insides are mangled and twisted like they are in a vice! Sara grabs me before I collapse; my whole body shacking beyond my control. My mind has shut down. It has closed off everything around me. The only thing I can hear is *"not expected to live"*, playing like a record on repeat. I go blank for a little bit and everything is in a haze.

The next thing I remember is Sara pulling over. I stumble out of the car to the side of the road. I fall to my knees and start to vomit. My heart feels like its fixing to explode and the pain is that of it being ripped from my chest. My complexion has drained from my face leaving it white as a sheet. I began to have a melt down sobbing uncontrollably.

"Oh God! Please!" I scream, "don't do this! I will do anything. I will take his place!"

I beg and plead with God to have mercy at one point bargain with the devil. I feel as though the life is slowly being sucked from my soul.

"I have to get to him! Take me to the hospital!" I shout.

She is trying everything in her power to console me.

"Breath Riley, please! Just breath!" she said, cradling me in her arms. "I will take you as soon as you calm down."

She begins to rock me like a child.

"I need to tell him I love him! I need him to know I love him more than life itself!" I cry out.

"He knows Riley. God! He knows," she whispers, as tears begin to fall from her eyes.

Her heart crumbles as she watches my world fall into a million pieces. She knows this will destroy my existence and be the death of me if he does not survive.

Sara helps me to the car and we head to the hospital.

"What are you going to do when we get their Riley? Are you going to tell his wife? Are you going to ask to see him? You know his whole family will be there," she said quietly.

"I don't know! My mind and heart is in torment!" I scream, placing my face in my hands hoping to drown out the sound of my cries.

Sara places her hand on my shoulder.

"We will figure it out when we get there," she whispers.

I'm trapped in purgatory; the unknowing is tormenting my soul. The thoughts flooding my mind are simply more than overload at this point. The two-hour drive to get to Jase will be the longest two hours of my life. The silence was so overbearing you could hear a pin drop. I get lost inside my thoughts, staring into space.

Chapter 11

I had so many decisions to make with no time to weigh on them. I sit in the parking lot of the hospital, instantly deciding that I can not be selfish any longer.

"I can't go in there Sara and bring more grief to his family by confessing my love. He is a hero in his daughter's eyes. No matter the out come I could never taint that. My need to be by his side would only take away the respect and admiration he deserves. This is my wrong, my cross to carry, not theirs! I just want to be close to him, close enough he can sense my presence," I said, breaking down.

"I will call the ICU waiting room and see if I can get an update," Sara said.

She puts the phone on speaker by the second ring, soft voice answers.

"Hello, I'm trying to get an update on Jase Carmichael," Sara states.

"This is his wife Carla, who's speaking?" says the voice.

"Ms. Carmichael, my name is Sara. My husband works for your husband. He has asked me to check on Jace for him."

"The situation is not good," Carla says. "The doctors only give him a ten- percent survival rate. The next seventy-two hours are going to be very critical. He has contacted the deadly virus Swine Flu. The survival rate is extremely low," she whispered.

"I am so sorry! I will be praying for your family!" Sara replied.

I open the car door and get out. Immediately, I began to dry heave. My world is caving in around me and I have no control over anything. I wipe my tears and collect myself the best I can.

"What are you thinking Riley?" Sara asks.

"I have to be closer to him," I said, as the tears swell back up.

We get on the elevator and the bell chimes to alert us that we have reached the third floor to the ICU. We walk down the hall, as despair drapes over me like a fur coat. At the end of the hall is the ICU waiting room. Off to the side is a dark deserted hallway that looks no longer in use. I glance at Sara and turn down the deserted hall, huddling quietly in the corner of its walls.

I pull my knees up to my chest to bury my head. I begin to talk to Jase in my mind. *I need you please don't leave me. You are the love of my life the very air I breath.* I'm praying with every ounce of my being that he can feel my presence. Sara sits next to me in complete silence. I look up at her tears in my eyes.

"Do you think he can feel my love?"

My voice crackling from all the emotion raging inside.

"Yes Riley! I believe with the bond you two have, he can hear your every cry!" she replies.

Fighting to hold back the tears. I fiercely watch the hall leading from the waiting room as people go in and out. I'm trying to profile their actions and listen intently to their conversations hoping to learn any information I can.

We have been sitting in this hallway for seventeen hours straight and it is now a quarter till four, in the morning. Sara goes down stairs and gets us something to drink. She calls Keith with hopes he could convince me to go home. When he arrives, he takes one look at me, and tells Sara to go home and get some rest.

"I'll stay here with Riley," he said softly.

Keith listens to me pray and beg God to wake Jase from his coma. He hears me gamble with everything, including my own life. He bends down in front of me and lifts my head.

"Let me take you home for a little while Riley. You need to get some rest and eat, before you make yourself sick."

The though of something happening and me not being here was torturing my mind.

"What if I go Keith and when I get back he's gone? If I leave I have no way of knowing."

"Sara said she would call and get an update as soon as you eat and get some rest," says Keith.

I have to will my feet to move. My mind knows I need the rest, but its having a hard time convincing my heart.

"Come on Riley we will come back I promise!" he says.

Holding my hand Keith continues to persuade me using logic and reason, step by step.

It's been seventy-two hours and no change. Sara calls once a day for an update and that is my only lifeline. He is still in a coma and on life support. His kidneys have failed, and he is not holding his own blood pressure. The medication to keep his heart beating has cut off all circulation to his legs. Gain green has begun to set up in his feet. I sit at night, under the window of the ICU, and talk to him.

"Use me Jase and fight! Let me be your every breath use my strength and hold on to me, let the rhythm of my heart beat sync with yours!"

The mental anguish has become more than I can handle.

There is not one part of the human sprit that is not being tested inside me; everything from my morals and beliefs to my strength and weakness. The aching in my heart is indescribable and I am angry with God!

"Don't punish him punish me, put me in his place!" I scream.

I feel a hand on my shoulder. I look up and there is Sara with tears rolling down her cheeks.

"What are you doing here? It's three o'clock in the morning you should be sleeping," I say.

She kneels down beside me.

"Riley, God is not punishing you! This is not your fault don't you know that?" she asks.

"It feels like he is," I mumble, with rage. "He could change this and heal him. He performs miracle everyday! Why won't he grant me one?"

"He has Riley, the love you found in Jace," says Sara.

"What! So he can take it away? Why would he do that? I have read the bible! Listened to the preacher about how great Gods love is, but this isn't love Sara!"

The tone in my voice is filled with hurt and anger.

"You don't mean that," Sara whispered softly.

"I feel so lost! The life is being sucked out of me. I'm dying inside and I don't know how to stop it," I said in defeat.

"I know, I watch it everyday," replied Sara, "and it scares the hell out of me! You haven't eaten anything and when you do it comes back up. I haven't seen you sleep in days! When you do drift off, you scream out in terror. I watch the guilt eat you alive and it breaks my heart! Will you please come home with me for a little while? Keith is waiting for us. He is going to stay with you until I get through at the office in the morning. Then we can call and see if there has been any change."

I am mentally and physically drained. My mind is so distraught I can't even remember what day it is. I agree only if she promises to bring me back that afternoon.

Once I get inside and sit on the couch, Keith brings me a pillow and blanket. He leans over and hugs my neck, kissing my cheek.

"Lay with me, rest those beautiful eyes," he states.

He begins to run his fingers through my hair. Flashbacks of Jase running his hands through my hair began to flood my mind. I can't hold back my emotions, the tears begin fall like rain. My body has no fight left. It gives way to the exhaustion as I drift off into a deep sleep. My mind drifts straight into the arms of Jase. The sweetest of dreams, only to be jolted into a nightmare! He is fading from my arms. There is nothing I can do. I scream, beg, and plead but he continues to disintegrate right before my eyes. I wake up in sheer panic!

"Something's wrong!" I scream with terror.

Chapter 12

Sara arrives but before she can get in the door I'm running toward the car. She stops me in the driveway.

"Hey, slow down," she grabs be by the arm.

"I need to get back, something's wrong! I feel it."

You can see my heart beating through my shirt.

"Calm down, let's go inside and we will call the hospital. Look at me Riley," she stated, in a demanding tone. "Come inside! Then I will take you, I promise!"

I'm antsy as I listen with intensity to the conversation between Sara and Carla. He has taken a turn for the worst! The doctors are at a lost. There is nothing else they can do. They are taking him in for emergency surgery to amputate his legs. Hoping this will help his heart and blood pressure stabilize. They advised us he could pass at any time.

"We have called in the family and our priest to say our good-byes," Carla states.

I grab Sara's keys off the table and take off. Keith chases after me screaming my name.

"Riley! Come back, please!"

I am running for my life, but have nowhere to run to! I spin out of the driveway, leaving Keith and Sara standing in despair.

I'm reckless and driving out of control. My mind is being flooded with memories. My heart is drowning in emotion. I can feel my spirit dying. I'm in a haze. I turn the car around. There is only one thing that can breathe life into me and save me from self-destruction. I have been angry with God, real angry. I know only his grace can only save me now! I've always turned to him, through out my life. God has always kept my head above water, although many times I felt unworthy. My relationship with him is complicated, but strong. I never realized he was leading me back to him when I turned around. I drove in total confusion for forty-five minutes. I ended up in the parking lot of a church. I get out of the car, falling to my knees. I began a conversation with God that would forever change my soul.

In the beginning I am angry and bitter. I unleash my fury, casting every stone possible. My tongue is lashing out and cutting to the core.

"If you're real, answer me!" I scream.

The rage I felt depleted my soul as I laid on the concrete weeping. The daylight has given way to darkness. I have spent hours provoking God and questioning his love. I get back on my knees with all the strength I have left, bowing my head. I beg for forgiveness while humbling my self before him.

"Without you, I am nothing. Please God! Have mercy on me! I was wrong for my relationship with Jase, but God I love him with every fiber of my being. He is the very air I breathe. The only happiness I've ever known. God if you will save him, I will right my wrong and walk away. I will trade my life for his. I can't live with the heavy burden of guilt that weights on my heart if he dies. The thought of that is too much for me to bare. This nightmare will haunt me for the rest of my life. I can carry my conviction and bare my cross as long as I know he is still here. My love for him will continue but must be done from afar. I plead for your mercy and pray you hear my cries."

I left every piece of my soul lying in that parking lot. The emptiness I felt was cold and harsh. I get in the car and stare out into the night. The stars are perfectly placed in the heavens. The moon steals their ambiance with its brilliant hue and luster. I'm too tired to think or concentrate any longer. I find myself lost in the still of the night. A sense of peace washes over me, cradling my soul. The serenity it brought was a safe haven that rocked me like a lullaby. I awake to the sunrise beaming its rays through the window of the car.

It hits me that Sara and Keith is probably sick with worry so I head back. I won't know anything about Jase until I get home and I am terrified. I look as though I have been to hell and back. My mascara out lines my cheeks from all the tears; my hair is unkept and frazzled. I get in the driveway as Keith comes out to the car. He walks to the passenger's side and gets in. He sits with me in silence placing his hand in mine.

"Please don't ever scare me like that again," he whispers, with tears in his eyes. "I have searched for you all night Riley."

I look at him, a single tear rolling down my cheek.

"I had to face my demons. I had to let go to survive," I whisper. "This is bigger than I am and beyond my control. I was not prepared for this battle Keith and it has broken down all my defenses."

"Where did you go? I looked everywhere! The hospital and every other place you run to when you want to escape," he asks.

"I was searching my soul, we will leave it at that," I reply. "I know now what I have to do."

I get inside and Sara knocks me over sobbing.

"I was so scared Riley! Don't ever leave me like that again!" she hollered.

"I'm so sorry Sara, I wont I promise. I need to check on Jase." Sara won't be able to call for a couple more hours so I tell them I just want to be alone. I go to my room and grab my paper and pen and spill my heart.

I never questioned it; you seemed so sincere,
Whatever bouts I had, you calmed my fear.

It wasn't something I would ordinarily do,
Yet it came so easy to trust in you.

So with disregard to all good advice,
I didn't hesitate or even think twice.

It was emotional suicide for this heart of mine,
But unknown to me I drank the wine.

It left the sweetest taste upon my lips,
And a magical feeling at my fingertips.

I could see the heavens as I soar through the sky,
An amazing rush an emotional high.

And the more you offered the more I tasted,
Now drunken by love I was emotionally wasted.

But as I go through withdrawals this is what I found,
Its much easier to go up, than it is to come down.

Because the dreaming is over and the reality is clear,
What you once desired becomes your worst fear.

From light to darkness that's how you fall,
From feeling everything to nothing at all.

What you use to believe in you no longer know,
It will steal your heart and scar your soul.

It will drive you crazy play games with your mind,
Taking you back from time to time.

Making you question where you belong,
It makes it feel right even though it is wrong.

A devastating battle and emotional fight,
There will be countless tears and sleepless nights.

Nearly loosing my sanity it almost drove me insane,
This deadly drug, running through my veins.

And I carry a scar that reminds me of,
How hard I fell from an overdose of love.

I have completely shut off my emotions. I feel so empty; I know I'm alive but I don't feel like it. My mind has blocked every thought and emotion to the point I don't remember what day it is. The turmoil has taken its toll. My body is in survival mode. I have been locked away in my room for hours when Sara knocks on the door.

"It's time Riley. We can call the hospital," she says.

I look up at her; she can see the terror on my face. *What if he didn't survive? Can I handle that?* I think to myself. I am frozen with fear.

"I will be in the living room when you are ready," said Sara.

She knows this phone call could be the one that kills my soul. I bow my head and silently pray. *God let your will be done but either way I will need your love to carry me through.* We as humans are scared of the unknown but for me it's the knowing that terrifies me.

I slowly head down the hall towards the living room. I have to force each step one by one. I feel like I am walking to my own hanging. The fear has paralyzed me and I am visibly shaken. My insides tremble and my stomach churns. I sit beside Sara as she holds my hand.

"I love you so much Riley! We are going to get through this together," she states.

I give a slight nod to show my acknowledgement.

"Are you ready?" she asks.

55

"I don't think I will ever be ready," I say, as the tears swell up in my eyes.

The sound of each button she pushes on the dial pad is like a dagger in my heart. The sound echo's in my head.

Chapter 13

The phone is on the third ring when my heart stops beating. I can only assume why no one is picking up. The dread is covering me like the plaque. Then a voice picks up. It's not Carla, she is who normally answers. I immediately panic.

"I'm calling to check on Jace Carmichael, is Carla available?" she asks.

"I will get her, please hold," says the stranger.

Sara looks at me saying, "This is a great sign Riley."

I can feel my heart beat again when Carla comes on the line.

"This is Carla," she said in a soft voice.

"I wanted to check on Jase and see how he is doing," said Sara.

The silence hovering and was so thick you couldn't have cut through it with a chainsaw.

"Sara, it's a miracle! Jase woke up out of his coma last night and is breathing on his own this morning. The doctors are medically stunned. He woke up screaming in terror the word Riley. The doctors sedated him so his body could rest," said Carla.

"Oh, thank God!" said Sara.

"He is not out of the woods yet," said Carla. "His kidneys are still not functioning and his blood pressure is low."

She pauses and takes a deep breath.

"He has yet to realize his legs have been amputated. He will be in devastation and have a hard time coming to grips with it. His complete recovery is far from over. I hate to cut you short but I need to be by his bedside in case he wakes up," Carla adds.

"I completely understand, thank you," said Sara.

I sit quietly as tears stream down my face. Sara can not contain her excitement when she hangs up. She is jumping around, hollering at the top of her lungs. There is no smile on my face and I am slightly coherent. She sits down beside me and lifts my head in her hands.

"This is a miracle Riley! God granted you your miracle!" she said.

"I know," I whisper.

"Then why are you so sad?" she asks.

I start to cry and then blurt, "I made a bargain with God Sara! I promised him if Jase survived I would walk away."

She stands up and walks around the coffee table. She is in complete shock and doesn't know what to say.

"I traded my life for his," I said sobbing.

"Why? Why would you make a promise like that? You belong with Jace and he belongs with you," she said in despair.

"If he did not survive Sara, I would not survive either," I state. "I could not except that I wouldn't be able to say goodbye or attend his funeral. Nothing Sara, I had nothing at all! It was killing me. I promised I would walk away once I knew he was out of the hospital and ok. I will have the opportunity to let him know how much I love him. I will at least know we share the same air."

"How are you going to do that Riley? It's going to kill you to not be able to see or talk to him," she said.

"I have to! I don't have a choice!" I cry out. "My suffering will never compare to what he has suffered. Our lives are forever changed Sara. There is a time and season for everything under the heavens. It's not my time or season!" I exclaim, in defeat.

My will is not Gods will and I have to except that. Jase and I can never be. My heart has just heard those words for the first time. It breaks into a million pieces over and over again. I am floored by my own words and have no idea how my heart and mind are completely out of sync. The battle has begun inside my soul. I will have to keep my self in check every second of the day. My thoughts must stay in control and cage my heart in order for me to honor my promise.

"This is the ultimate affliction," Sara states. "I'm scared of what this promise is going to do to you!"

She hugs me and I drench her shirt with my tears.

"I'm scared to," I whisper.

I go back to my room and let it all soak in. I am grateful Jase will pull through yet overwhelmed with sadness. I can't picture life without him. He is the very air I breathe every beat of my heart. What will become of this empty shell that was once full of life? I have no answers to my questions and never will; this is greater than I am able to conceive and its something I may never understand. The one thing that I do know is that for a moment of time in my life I had heaven on earth. I found my one true love. It was everything love is supposed to be. I found that in Jase. I tell Sara to go home.

"I'm going to be ok!" I said. "You have done enough and I am so grateful to have you and Keith by my side. It's a terrifying thought of where I would be right now if I didn't have you!"

I grab her and hug her tight.

"I'm just a call away Riley! Don't hesitate day or night," she said.

"I know Sara. I might have to take you up on that," I reply, as a tear rolls down my cheek.

Sara will still be my only lifeline to Jase until he is able to leave the ICU.

I go out on the porch to get some fresh air. The breeze sweeps over me bringing a slight chill to my skin. The heavens are lit up like a Christmas tree. The stars twinkle and dance across the sky. The moon is big and full demanding attention. I decide to drive to the hospital and have a heart to heart conversation with Jace. I know it sounds crazy but I pray that he can feel my love; I talk to him often. It's all I have. If I keep it all bottled up inside I will self-destruct. I am a ticking time bomb; waiting to explode with these bottled up emotions. My only release is to pray to God, talk to Jace, or write for hours. There is a hurricane brewing in the depths of this ragging sea called my soul and like a dam I have to open the floodgates to minimize the destruction.

On the drive I plug in my I-Pod getting lost in the songs. They are some of Jace and my favorites. They take me on a trip down memory lane. I swear I can feel him with me sometimes. When I close my eyes I can feel his touch, hear his voice, and feel his breath on my skin. It's comforting and bitter sweet rolled into one. I park my car and ride the elevator to the third floor. I disappear into the darkness and hover in my corner. I began my conversation.

"They should name this wing Riley's hall. I'm starting to get a little too comfortable here Jace. You need to quit procrastinating and get yourself together." I can't help but smile. "I don't know if you ever realized this but you where my whole world. I'm not even sure there are words to describe the depth in which I love you! I miss the sound of your voice. That alone was enough to calm my soul. You have a way with me that brings me to life. You complete me and make me whole," I said. My voice cracks and I begin to cry. "I would take your place if I could. I wish I could just see you, hold you and take your pain away. I feel so helpless and desperate," I said. I have my head buried in my knees sobbing uncontrollably by this point.

"He's getting stronger and I'm sure he feels the same!"

I stand up and look down the hallway. I see a slim figured female with dark hair disappear around the corner. I stand there frozen in disbelief. I can only wonder how long she had been listening and if she had seen me here before.

I have never met Carla but my intuition tells me she knows who I am. I pull myself together and head toward the elevator. I get to the parking lot when I see the mysterious women and a young lady talking. I can see that her long brown hair and emerald eyes are the same features as Jace. I have no way to be sure but I believe this is the princess that holds the heart of Jace Carmichael. I have no choice but to over hear the young ladies conversation. She talks about her love for her father and how she can't wait till he comes home. This only confirms my earlier thoughts. Carla has over heard me and knows of the relationship between Jace and myself. I hurry to my car with a heavy heart. I feel sick at my stomach. I never wanted to hurt her any more than she is already. Finding this out is just adding more poison to an already toxic situation!

Chapter 14

It's been two days since I've been to the hospital. I can not bring myself to risk another encounter with his family. That night has played over and over in my mind. I have been doing a lot of soul searching and realize how wrong I was in my relationship with Jase. I am over whelmed with conviction. I began to write.

Late at night I would gaze at the stars,
The seemed so close yet so far.

Was there something out there waiting for me,
A laid out plan my destiny.

Then in the distant something caught my eye,
A shooting star to my surprise.

Straight from the heavens I watched it fall,
A wish to be granted so I wished for it all.

Someone to love for which I could depend,
Not just a lover but also a friend.

Someone to have someone to hold,
Someone to give my heart to and share my soul.

It didn't take long before I knew,
My wish had been granted and it was you.

Everything I've wanted the greatest love I've known,
So how could it be I couldn't call you my own.

It was a devastating mistake in destiny's plan,
For whatever reasons I may never understand.

Why this happened or how it could be,
The wish had been granted just not for me.

I was blinded by love but now the vision is clear,
Only to clarify my worst fears.

The star I was holding belong to someone else,
Someone who loves it as much as myself.

So everything I wanted was never mine,
Not now or at any time.

Nothing can change the way things are,
For I have been wishing on someone else's star.

The more time that goes by, the more I come to grips with the big picture. I lay down my pen and cry myself to sleep.

The next morning I report to work at my normal time. I have not faced my coworkers for very long in the last two months. I did most of my work from home and Sara carried a major load. I feel a little uncomfortable at first. I know Sara had to tell them something but I don't know how much they know. No one confronts me and everyone is kind. Sara comes in and closes the office door.

"How are you holding up?" she asks, with a smile. "I have been trying to give you some breathing room. I'm sure you have had more of Keith and me than you wanted over the last two months."

"I'm getting better," I reply.

"You had me so scared Riley! I thought for sure you where going to," she pauses.

"Nope! I couldn't let you off the hook that easy. You and Keith are stuck with me," I say smiling.

"I will take it," Sara said hugging my neck.

I tell Sara about my event at the hospital and how it torments my mind.

"I never wanted to hurt anyone but at the same time I cant deny my love for him either. The whole situation is a horrific tragedy," I said.

"You're only human Riley. You made a mistake, that's all!" she exclaims.

"Mistake? I will never consider Jace a mistake! He is the only thing that brought me to life! How could that be considered a mistake?" I ask.

"I didn't mean it the way it sounded," she replied.

"I'm sorry Sara, I'm just a complete mess. My emotion runs from one extreme to the other. I get confused and mangled. One minute I have this overwhelming desire to break into his room and confess my love; not caring who knows or who it hurts. Selfish I know," I said. "Then a strong conviction of guilt takes over the next minute. I can only imagine all the hurt I must have caused his wife. What a great woman she must be to try and comfort me at the hospital in her time of despair. She felt compassion for me and I am so unworthy. My mind is in a battle and my heart is twisted."

Sara squeezes my hand saying, "Your going to get though this!"

Sara calls the hospital for an update and things are looking up. Jase is functioning on his own. Everything's good besides his kidneys. He will stay on dialysis and the doctors said that in time they might begin to work on there own. He will be moved from ICU in a couple days as long as he keeps improving. It breaks my heart that I can only imagine the mental torture he has to endure. This hasn't gotten any easier for me. I still can't hold down food so I'm losing weight like crazy. I look like a waking zombie, sleep deprived doesn't even cover it. I'm forgetful and can't concentrate my mind is fixated on how Jace is doing. I try to keep some sort of repetition going though out my day to keep from going crazy. I'm still not able to keep my emotions in check. I find myself burst into tears out of no where. I know my time is coming to an end and that weighs heavy on my shoulders. Once Jace is well enough to leave the hospital I can no longer have contact with him. The thought of that in its self hits me dead on like a truck. I don't know that I'm strong enough to handle the ending effect that this will have on me.

Chapter 15

Jace spent twelve weeks in ICU before he was moved to a regular room. He is now going through physical therapy to strengthen his body. He will be in a wheel chair until he gets his prosthetics. He has a long road to complete recovery. He will have to learn to walk again. I have to prepare myself for the first real conversation with him today. Sara comes to the house for lunch and to call the hospital.

"Are you ready for this Riley?" she asks.

"Can anyone be prepared for this?" I reply.

My emotions are like a raging sea but I know I have to keep them under control. The phone rings twice and I hear his voice for the first time in so long.

"Hello?" he answers.

The tears begin to stream instantly down my face. The sound of his voice electrifies my soul.

"Hello," I reply in a soft tone.

I try to hide the fact I'm in tears so I don't upset him.

"Riley, is that you?" he asks.

You can hear the sadness in his voice.

"Yes Jace, its me! I love you so much!" I blurt out.

I have wanted to tell him this for so long. The emotion is so powerful there is no way to hold it back; I break down sobbing.

He whispers softly, "They took my legs. I'm a broken man."

I'm being torn into I can feel his anguish and despair.

"I'm so sorry," I whisper. "I'm so sorry."

I can tell he is weeping and I would give anything to cradle him and tell him it will be ok.

"You really scared me! I need you to concentrate on getting well," I said.

I'm trying to defuse the conversation about his legs to keep his mind off of that. I can tell it has sent him into a deep depression.

"I love you more that life itself Jace you know that right?" The other end of the line becomes silent.

"Right?" I ask.

"You wont anymore," he said. "I look like a freak Riley!"

64

"I can't believe you would even think like that Jace!" I holler. "I don't care if you have legs! I love who you are. Everything about you and there is nothing that will ever change that!"

"I have to go Riley. I will talk to you later," he replies, as the phone goes dead.

I am crushed. The turmoil he has to endure scares me. I know he won't ever be the same; losing his legs will plaque him for the rest of his life. I'm not sure its possible to make him understand my love for him. It goes much deeper than the outer shell. I love his soul and just want to be able to breathe the same air.

"He's in shock and doesn't mean to be so short," said Sara. "I'm sorry Riley. I know this is killing you to watch him suffer."

"I'm just grateful he's alive. Grateful that I able to hear his voice," I whisper.

The sadness dwelling in my eyes weighed heavy on Sara's heart. She was enduring the same thing I am. She watches me die a little more each day and there is nothing she can do to stop it. Jace cannot except the hand he has been dealt and he slips further and further into depression. I try to keep his spirits up but can't break through his walls. I have not told Jace about the promise I made. It would only cause more turmoil and I need him to get well. I have to know he is going to be ok for me to survive.

The more the days pass, the stronger Jace is getting. It's been six days since he was moved to a room and his kidneys have begun working on their own. I am running out of time. The doctors said he could go home in a few more days. I have come to be thankful for my one call a day. The emotional torture I feel is indescribable. How do you walk away from the one thing that brings you to life? Just the sound of his voice tames the turbulence in my soul. I truly believe that my love for Jace will be a life sentence. He has imprinted my heart.

Chapter 16

The day has come and Jace has been cleared to go home. The announcement thrusts me into darkness. I've been here before; it's cold and scary with no mercy to be found. I must begin the separation to hold up to my end of the deal. I don't know how your suppose to choose between life and death. I can feel the noose tightening around my neck.

"I will come see you Riley, as soon as I learn to walk," he said. "It might be a while but I'm coming for you."

I have shed enough tears to dry up the wetlands but they keep falling like rain. Those word cut like a knife. I have been waiting for eleven years now there will be no end to my wait. I have a lifetime and will still be without Jace Carmichael.

"You will be running before you know it," I reply. "You are an inspiration to everyone that knows you and you're my hero! You are the chosen one a living miracle," I state.

It's been three days since I've talked to Jace. He sends me texts but I answer back every now and then.

Damn you Riley! Why won't you talk to me?

Your are ashamed of me now. Aren't you?

I'm not good enough for you know that I'm crippled is that it?

That is the furthest thing from the truth but how can I convince him of that? I reply back!

My god Jace you know me better than that or at least I thought you did. I've just been really busy with work.

I am hoping his anger pulls him away from me with out me having to push him away. I knew if he were able to confront me face to face, my love for him would win. I would break my promise to God! Sara tries to perk up my spirits by inviting me to Mackie's for lunch.

"Come on Riley! Everyone misses you and it's on me," she said. "We can get your favorite."

"You know I'm a sucker for the chips and salsa," I said, with a smile. "It will have to be a late lunch. I have something I have to do first and then run to the post office. I will call you when I'm on my way."

"That's a deal!" she screeched.

We head out our separate ways. I head to my house. I have decided to write Jace a letter to explain my distance.

I pull up in the drive. My heart is in a million pieces; I don't know that I can even find the words to express what I feel. I sit at the table and stare at the pen and paper. There are so many things I want to say. I want him to know that it's a higher power. Its is no longer my will, but Gods will. I will never be able to write again. Putting that pen to the paper was the hardest thing I will ever do. My eyes are filled with tears and my hands are shaking.

> *My love,*
>
> *You are everything to me. I have never believed in fairytales but because of you, I lived one. You are my one true love, my soul mate. I never want you to question or doubt my love. When I heard you where not suppose to live it put me in a place I was not prepared for. It shook me visibly to the core of my soul. I was tied between my own desires and what was right. I desired to bust through that door and confess my unwavering love. Give you my last breath and take your place. Then on the other hand if you did not survive I would have tarnished the love of a hero in your daughter's eyes. I could not allow that and had to put aside my selfish ways. I bargained with the devil and pleaded with God! The toll it was taking on me left me lifeless. I was dying along with you. I fell to my knees and I promised God I would right my wrongs and walk away if you survived. Knowing this would condemn me to a life a hell. I will never get to touch you, feel your breath on my skin, see your face, or hear your laughter. The voice that calmed my soul would no longer be leaving me to drown in raging waters, stripping me of the air I breath. So before you question my love. I want you to know this. I gave my life for yours; without you I am a empty shell. You have a second chance, use it wisely Jace. Love with all your heart and be humble. Take nothing for granted and find*

*happiness in the simple things. You will forever hold
my heart. I will love you for eternity.*

Forever yours,
Riley Davis

I feel something dying inside me with every line I write. I can barely see through my swollen eyes. I seal the envelope and drive to the post office. I seal my fate as I watch it fall into the box. I call Sara and tell her I'm on my way. I drive off broken.

Chapter 17

The instance I drove by and seen the car I knew it was Riley. My heart sinks as I look at the mangled cars. I pull over and run across the street before being stopped by a police officer. I scream out her name and it echoes in my mind. I see the helicopter land and watch as they load her.

"Where are they taking her?" I scream.

"Oak Ridge Hospital," the officer replies.

I jump in my car and call Keith. I am frantic and Keith can't make since of a word I say.

"Its Riley! Meet me at Oak Ridge," I scream in terror.

The doctors stop me in the hall and tell me her injuries are fatal. I ask to see her to say my good-byes. With each step I could feel the breaking of my heart. I sit in silence at her beside and run my fingers through her hair. Her lifeless body is battered and bruised. I tell her I love her for the last time and kiss her forehead. They come and wheel her away. I hear Keith running down the hall screaming her name. He enters the room and falls to his knees.

"Where is she Sara?"

I kneel beside him and whisper, "She's gone."

You could hear the whaling echoing through the halls.

"What happened to her Sara?" asks Keith.

"She died from a broken heart," I whispered softly.

The funeral was beautiful. Riley left her mark on the world. Everyone she encountered loved her. Keith and I head over to go through her things. We cry and we laugh as everything we look at reminds us a moment we all shared. I pick up a picture off the shelf and lose control. Sobbing I fall to my knees. Keith comes over to console me when a car pulls in the drive. A deep voice bellows out Riley's name. I run to the door and standing at the bottom of the stairs is Jace with a letter in his hands.

"Go get Riley!" he demands. "Tell her I made it back to her. I'm never going to let her go!"

I can't utter a word and the tears began to stream down my face. Keith comes to the door and stands in silence.

"What's going on?" Jace hollers. "Where is she?"

You can see the terror in his eyes.

"She's gone," I choke.

"Gone where?" Jace replies.

"She died Monday in an accident on here way from the post office," Keith whispers. "That day will forever be ingrained in my mind."

Jace opens the letter and stagers to the porch. The blood hurling scream echo's in my mind today.

"God no!" he shouts. "No! Bring her back and take me!" he screams.

Love is patient, love is kind. It does not envy, it does not boast, it is not proud. It does not dishonor others, it is not self-seeking, it is not easily angered, it keeps no record wrongs. Love does not delight in evil but rejoices with the truth. It always protects, always trusts, always hopes, and always perseveres. Love never fails. But where there are prophecies, they will cease; where there are tongues, they will be stilled; where there is knowledge, it will pass away.

1 Corinthians 13:4-8

About the Author

An avid radio personality, P.D. Fitzgerald was born in Dallas, Tx on November 1970. The fourth of five girls, she knew at a young age that competition in this world was Fierce. With the Fire embedded within her, she began writing poems and short stories in her teenage years as a hobby. Much to her delight, she was awarded for a published poem by The National Library of Poetry in 2005. Her flair for writing enables her to relate to readers and entice them in with her compassionate and enthralling works of literature.

The mother of two grown children, it was only logical that P.D. take her writing one step further to fulfill her dream. Each and every word she writes captures the embodiment of love, lust and passion as it was meant to be articulated to her readers. With sheer passion pouring from every page, she is able to capture the purity of true love and the steamy passion that we all yearn for. She will leave your head spinning and have you counting the days until hernext release.

Printed in the United States
By Bookmasters